midnight or so like always. Bailey and I decided to sleep in her room together that last night and talked about how great our senior year was going to be. We also talked about where we'd get an apartment when I came back the next summer. I was excited by that prospect. I knew then there was *nothing* that would ever stand in mine and Kevin's way again. We had made it through Geoffrey, Clarice, Lori, me going with Jax and then moving to Oklahoma and then Corpus Christi, along with everything else that seemed to constantly be in our way the last 4 ½ years.

When I realized it was 1 a.m. I began to worry that Kevin would stand me up again like he'd done the last time I'd been home. Bailey began to get sleepy even though she skipped her medicine that night so we could stay up late and talk. Soon she was breathing softly and I was straining to hear a tap on the glass. I finally picked up the phone and dialed Kevin's number. I was shocked when it was busy. I waited about 15 minutes and tried it again and it was busy still. I felt my heart begin to fall as I realized that he was either avoiding me or maybe he was on the phone with Jackie. No matter which one it meant he wouldn't be coming to Bailey's like he'd said the night before.

My mind skipped to our kiss goodbye the night before again. I began to worry that it was really a goodbye *for real*, forever kind of kiss. The more I lay there thinking about it, the more I finally realized that what I'd taken for granted as the most passionate kiss Kevin ever gave me, was also the one that he was giving me to send me away. He was hoping I didn't come back next year. I thought about every word he'd said to me and thought about how he'd told me he loved me. I felt a large lump as it began to choke me up. I rolled over with my back to Bailey and let the hot tears slide out and cried until I was asleep. The morning got there way too quickly.

During my bus trip home I replayed that last kiss over and over and thought about what he'd told me. I wondered if he really didn't want me to come back, or if he was just trying to get me to move on because he thought he was such a loser. I decided that he would see when I came back the next summer that *I* was serious. This time he hadn't told me not to contact him, so I was going to write to him when I got home and tell him that he could ignore me all year long if he wanted to, but when I said I was coming back, *I meant it*. I hoped he'd know how serious I was.

Getting home to Corpus wasn't very monumental to me except I was depressed. I was more depressed than I ever remembered being and didn't even want to go anywhere when I got home. I just wanted to stay home the first couple of days I was back and barely even came out of my room. I spent the day in my night shirt and shorts and lay in bed all day. I felt like I had a broken heart in some ways. I also just felt depressed over life in general. I couldn't put my finger on why. On Wednesday I got a letter in the mail from Bailey. I was excited because she hardly ever wrote anymore. If I was getting it on Wednesday it meant she wrote it and mailed it by Monday. I was hoping she was writing to tell me she'd broken up with creepy Casey!

Dear Lala,

I'm crying as I write this letter because I know how much it is going to hurt you and I wouldn't hurt you for anything in the world. There is no easy way to write it so I'm just going to say it and just know I'm so sorry.

Kevin called me on Sunday morning after I took you to the bus station. He told me to write to you and let you know that he's sorry he didn't come over before you left. He didn't want to mislead you because something really bad has happened.

He is getting married this weekend to Jackie. She is pregnant. I'm so sorry, Lala! Please call me if you need to talk to me. Call collect. I'll pay Glenda back. Just know that I never wanted to write this letter to you. He wants you to move on. He said to tell you that what he told you on Friday night he meant. He said you'd know what he was talking about. Something about when he

TREBETHERICK

TREBETHERICK

A Story of North Cornwall

as written by one David Rounsevall
of the Parish of St. Enodoc
in that County

GRATIANA CHANTER

Edited and with an introduction by
Gina R. Collia

NEZU
PRESS

Published by Nezu Press
Queensgate House,
48 Queen Street,
Exeter, Devon,
EX4 3SR,
United Kingdom.

This edition published 2024

Trebetherick first published by Francesco Giannini & Figli.,
Napoli, 1913.

ISBN-13: 978-1-7393921-9-2

In the interest of preservation, the punctuation and spelling of the original first edition text have been maintained, and the original formatting has been used wherever possible. A number of local dialect words and phrases appear throughout this work, and each is translated within a footnote upon its first appearance. Publisher errors and spelling inconsistencies have been silently corrected.

'No Sound but of the Raging Sea', by Gratiana Chanter, from *The Rainbow Garden.*

CONTENTS

Gratiana Chanter

The Girl's Dream Annual, 1903.

Gratiana Chanter
'A Typical Devon Daughter'
by Gina R. Collia

Gratiana Chanter was born at the vicarage in Ilfracombe, North Devon, on 9 May 1857, the fifth child of Rev. John Mill Chanter (1808-1893) and his wife, Charlotte (née Kingsley, 1827-1882).[1] Charlotte Chanter, fearless fern-hunter and author of *Ferny Combes*, was born in Barnack, Cambridgeshire,[2] to Charles Kingsley (1781-1860) and his wife, Mary (née Lucas, 1787-1873),[3] but she spent the early years of her childhood in Clovelly, forty-odd miles southwest of Ilfracombe, where her father served as curate and then rector.[4] Charlotte's eldest brother, also called Charles Kingsley (1819-1875), was the well-known author of *Westward Ho!* and *The Water-Babies*, and her youngest brother, Henry, was the author of *The Recollections of Geoffry Hamlyn* and *Ravenshoe.*

John Mill Chanter, the third son of Rev. William Chanter (1766-1859) and his wife, Mary (née Wolferstan, 1770-1824), was born at the parsonage in Hartland, Devon,[5] where the scenery is 'grand, marvellous, and awful; the thunder of the Atlantic is for ever in one's ears; the salt spray in one's face, glorious, invigorating, and inspiring'.[6] And it was in Hartland, a next-door neighbour to Clovelly, that John spent his childhood days, in a land 'full of many a wild story of smuggling, wrecking, and the supernatural.'[7] He was appointed vicar of Ilfracombe in April 1836,[8] and on 8 May he 'read himself in'.[9]

The Kingsleys had first made the acquaintance of John Mill Chanter in 1830.[10] During the following years, with the Kingsleys living in Clovelly and John and his family residing in neighbouring

Hartland, it was natural that they should see something of each other. When the Kingsleys left Clovelly for Chelsea in 1836, they continued to visit North Devon when the opportunity arose, and in January 1848 they visited Ilfracombe.[11] Charlotte, then twenty years old, and John, twenty years her senior, had a great deal in common. They shared an intense love of nature and, along with Charlotte's brother Charles, spent a considerable amount of time exploring Ilfracombe and the surrounding areas.

> ' "I remember" (said a dear old friend) "…Miss Kingsley, had a class of girls; I was one of them, and Mr. Charles would often come in when we were there, and make us all laugh with his funny, quaint sayings. Long expeditions they took together, Miss Kingsley, Charles, and the Vicar, mostly on horseback (for they were all at home in the saddle) away to little Trentishoe, or beautiful Lynton and Lynmouth, or the other way to Braunton Burrows, on botanising excursions, or for a long stretching gallop across the yellow sands of

Ilfracombe Town and Harbour, published by Fisher, Son & Co., 1830.

Ilfracombe Vicarage, by Gratiana Chanter, from *Wanderings in North Devon.*

> Woollacombe to Croyde, with the fragrant scent from the brown seaweed in their faces. Pleasant days indeed they must have been." '[12]

The following year, on 10 May 1849, John and Charlotte were married at Clifton Church, Gloucestershire, after which the couple returned to Ilfracombe vicarage, where they would remain together for the next thirty-three years.[13]

Holy Trinity Church, from *Twenty-Four Views of Ilfracombe* by J. Gadsby, c. 1875.

When John Mill Chanter first took on the role of vicar of Ilfracombe, the parish church, Holy Trinity, was in a terrible state; the pews were full of woodworm, the windows rattled in their frames, and the stones along the aisles had been so badly laid that the foul odour from those buried beneath found its way into the church itself.[14] The vicarage and its garden were in as sorry a state as the parish church. The house had been home to countless rodents for years; in fact, the very first soul to greet him when he arrived at his new home was a very large rat.[15] When it rained, the kitchen floor 'used to be an inch or two deep in water, so that the maids were obliged to trot about in pattens.'[16] And the garden was an overgrown wilderness, surrounded by derelict barns. John set to work right away; the barns were removed, 'the rats were dismissed', and he planted every tree and shrub in the vicarage garden himself.[17]

The vicarage was a 'long low house with a buff coloured face and deep finely slated roof, not always even, but gently undulating as if its old beams had wearied with keeping the horizontal for so many centuries, and had lowered their aching arms to a more restful position.'[18] Within the oldest part of the house—above the kitchen, which was thought to have been the original mansion house's entrance hall—there was a haunted room; it was used as a lumber room as all refused to sleep in it.[19] The ghosts were said to be those of two pretty children, murdered by their uncle for their money, who wandered the room and sighed.[20]

The Chanters' first child and only son, Kingsley, was born on 24 March 1850.[21] Mary Geraldine arrived the following year, on 5 June.[22] Then came Louisa Cadogan (15 March 1853),[23] Mabilla (15 November 1854),[24] and Gratiana (9 May 1857).[25] Katherine Stanley was born two years after Gratiana, on 19 February 1859,[26] and the Chanters' final child Charlotte Joyce, arrived four years later, on 28 June 1863.[27]

South Side of Vicarage, by Gratiana Chanter, from *Wanderings in North Devon.*

Since becoming vicar of Ilfracombe, in addition to providing church services, directing the renovation of Holy Trinity, and raising funds for the construction of a new church to serve the town's increasing population, John had held classes at the vicarage for both girls and boys, day and Sunday school classes 'in the tumble-down room over the Market', and he had an infant school at the Quay.[28] He taught the schoolmistress himself, to so high a standard that she satisfied the school inspectors for forty years.[29] And he and Charlotte provided all of their own children with an education; various newspaper reports listed their children's achievements in school examinations.[30]

The vicar's 'quiet humour and power of telling a good story' made him a delightful companion for his children,[31] and Charlotte, who 'had an endless stock of delightful German legends and fairy-tales at her fingers' ends', captivated them with tales of goblins, water nymphs, Devon pixies, and the headless Mullacott Ghost.[32] In 1858, the Chanters' collections of tales for children, *Jack Frost and Betty Snow*, was published by Griffith and Farran. The stories within the small volume, about 'the different dogs, cats, and birds, who had from time to time formed part of their household',[33] were dedicated to Kingsley, who was then eight years old, 'for whom they were written to enliven the weariness of a rainy week'.[34]

Charlotte and John Chanter were keen naturalists, and they encouraged their children to take an interest in the natural world around them. They possessed an adventurous spirit and weren't afraid to get their hands dirty; they enjoyed exploring uncharted territory, and their explorations around the Devonshire countryside often required that they 'rough it'.[35] The people of Ilfracombe were very much aware of the Chanters' great interest in the local flora and fauna, and the vicar was considered 'an authority on such matters'.[36] On one occasion, a gentleman walking on the beach at the Tunnels encountered what he thought was 'a large lump of meat' between some rocks and gave it a poke with his stick. When, in response, the 'impolite mass of blubber' spurted him with water, onlookers suggested a consultation with the vicar of Ilfracombe was in order. John, with the assistance of Rev. J. C. Lewis, performed an examination and pronounced it to be 'a fine young "octopus" '.[37]

Gratiana inherited her parents' passionate love of nature. She also inherited their spirit of adventure. From her mother, 'a brilliant and cultured woman', she inherited her story-telling ability; from her father, great skill with a fishing rod.[38] The vicar was a keen angler; from childhood he had been 'devoted to the gentle art of "fishing." '[39] In adulthood, there was nothing he loved more than to 'wander rod in hand up some moorland valley, enticing the speckled trout from his pebbly nook'.[40] Gratiana's childhood was 'a record of a healthy, happy, out-of-door life', spent wandering about the North Devon countryside, 'up and down the lovely moorland trout streams', with her father, 'one of the most noted fishermen of his day'.[41] She, like her father, was an expert angler and as a child sometimes returned home after a day's fishing with 'a basket of seventy trout'.[42] Many years later, when Gratiana spoke of her childhood to the *Girl's Realm Annual*—of her love of nature, her writing, her drawing and painting, and her ability to cross an Exmoor bog unharmed—she was pronounced 'a typical daughter of Devon'.[43]

Also from her father, Gratiana inherited a love of music; the vicar's family, on his mother's side, were famous for their singing voices,[44] and the vicar himself was president of the Ilfracombe Choral Society from 1875 to 1888.[45] Gratiana, her father, and her sisters—particularly Louisa, who was generally referred to as Lilian or Lily—regularly performed at concerts and amateur theatricals held at Holy Trinity, the town hall, local schools, and the Ilfracombe Battery of the 1st Devon Artillery of Volunteers;[46] Gratiana, being a talented artist, also painted the scenery for some performances.[47]

In October 1868, Gratiana and her family visited Morwenstow,

Tonacombe Manor, from a drawing by J. Ley Pethybridge, c. 1910.

located about ten miles to the south of the vicar's childhood home in Hartland. Gratiana described Tonacombe Manor, the fine medieval house where she and her family stayed, as 'suggestive of everything that was mysterious and delightful.'[48] One of Tonacombe's bedrooms was haunted by a ghost called Zachary, 'a delightful place to creep to in the twilight, and peep through the keyhole, with the expectation of witnessing the ghostly Zachary performing ghostly deeds'.[49] An external stone staircase led from a little courtyard to the haunted chamber.[50] During their visit, there were many storms, and 'miles inland could be heard the raging of the sea… a green black mountain of water, rounding and rolling on, ever gathering in force and size as it nears the bristling shore and boulder-laden beach'.[51] The Chanters spent most of their time on the cliffs or under them, looking for Cornish diamonds.[52]

The following year, when Gratiana was twelve years old, her father bought the Millslade Inn, in the village of Brendon, near Lynton, and converted it into a private residence.[53] The Chanters had stayed at the inn from time to time over the years, to have access to the nearby East Lyn river for trout fishing, and after their purchase of it their summer holidays were always 'passed amongst the wooded vales, and breezy moorlands with which it is surrounded.'[54] They travelled to Millslade in one of Colwill's "three-horse breaks", driving through Ilfracombe, 'with a farewell look at the harbour', and then on to Hele Bay, Watermouth, Combe Martin, Parracombe—where tea was taken at the Fox and Goose[55]—along Dean Steep to Barbrook Mill, then on to Lynton, Countisbury, and finally Brendon.[56] Gratiana described the house as 'not a handsome one, but a comfortable and cosy home, situated in a singularly beautiful position'.[57] The area was, and still is, very popular amongst anglers and artists.

On 2 December 1869, Gratiana's only brother, Kingsley, enlisted in the Merchant Navy. One year later, he deserted.[58] He did not return to England, and Gratiana had not seen her brother for more than five years when, in January 1875, while the vicar was suffering from a severe attack of bronchitis,[59] the Chanters received news that Kingsley was dead.[60] He had been travelling on an American steamer when, having fallen or been washed overboard, he drowned 'in the element he always loved so well'; according to the *Ilfracombe Chronicle*, 'the free-hearted youth', who

Millslade, by Gratiana Chanter, from *Wanderings in North Devon.*

appears to have been well liked, was 'a victim to his too great love of adventure'.[61]

By the time of Kingsley's death, Gratiana's mother was seriously ill. She suffered from chronic myelitis—chronic inflammation of the spinal cord[62]—the common symptoms of which include sensations of numbness or tingling, pain, fatigue, and muscle weakness; at the end of the nineteenth century, chronic myelitis would usually result in complete paralysis and, after a prolonged and painful illness, death.[63] Her physician would have required her to 'keep in a horizontal position' and 'never lie on the back'.[64] Charlotte accompanied her family on a holiday visit to Millslade for the last time in the summer of 1877.[65]

Charlotte Chanter died at Ilfracombe vicarage on 19 March 1882; Gratiana was twenty-four years old at the time.[66] During the morning before Charlotte's burial, which took place five days later, 'the bells of the Parish Church rang out muffled peals', and throughout the town shops were closed and blinds were drawn 'as a token of respect for the deceased lady's memory'.[67] During the funeral service the church was crowded,[68] and a hundred or so of the town's inhabitants attended the burial. She was buried 'amid general manifestation of sorrow' in a vault constructed 'in the new portion of the churchyard' at Holy Trinity.[69]

For the next four years, John Chanter, continued as vicar of Ilfracombe, and he and his daughters remained at Ilfracombe vicarage.[70] However, in November 1886 Edward Henry Bickersteth, the Bishop of Exeter, suggested that John, being then seventy-eight years old, should resign on account of his age.[71] The vicar's parishioners were wholly in favour of him remaining in his post, and it appears that the vicar himself was entirely willing to continue his work, but the bishop favoured retirement. During the first week of December, the vicar tendered his resignation; it was accepted immediately.[72] Before the year was out, the bishop had offered the living of Ilfracombe to John's replacement.[73] A public meeting was held in March 1887 to discuss the collection of subscriptions for a testimonial to the vicar's fifty-one years of faithful service,[74] and in March the following year John was presented with a silver salver and a purse of one hundred guineas.[75] By the beginning of the following year, he and his daughters had left Ilfracombe and moved permanently to Millslade.

In September 1887, Gratiana's memoir of her father, *Wanderings in North Devon: Being Records and Reminiscences in the Life of John Mill Chanter, M. A., Oxon, 51 Years Vicar of Ilfracombe*, was published by Twiss & Son of Ilfracombe. In addition to providing a vivid picture of her father's life, and of her own childhood, Gratiana produced a number of drawings to illustrate the book.[76] 'The whole volume,' wrote the 'local literature' reporter for the *North Devon Journal*, 'teems with scenes, stories and occurrences which have an inexhaustible interest for the people of North Devon' and for the tourists who 'flock hither in the summer's prime.'[77]

Rev. John Mill Chanter, 1887, from *Wanderings in North Devon.*

John Mill Chanter died at Millslade at the age of eighty-four on 11 February 1893.[78] The night before his funeral, his body was taken from Brendon to Ilfracombe, 'escorted by an immense crowd', and his coffin remained in Holy Trinity's chancel overnight, watched over by devoted members of the late vicar's congregation.[79] Shortly before his funeral, which was attended by about 1,300 mourners, the bells rang a muffled peal.[80] He was laid to rest alongside his late wife on 16 February.[81] The following year, a new lych gate was erected at Holy Trinity as a memorial to the late vicar; the dedication ceremony took place on 18 October 1894.[82]

By the time of the vicar's death, Gratiana's eldest sister, Mary, and her youngest, Charlotte, had become Sisters of Mercy,[83] and Lily had married Rev. James Frederic Vallings and was living in Hampshire.[84] Only Gratiana, Mabilla and Katherine remained at Millslade. The three sisters took an active interest in their local community and were 'always ready to help in any entertainment for the benefit of the parish'; they undertook sole management of the Brendon Men's Club, and they regularly took part in concerts that were held at the local schoolroom in aid of that institution.[85]

The lych gate dedicated to the memory of John Mill Chanter.

In November 1892, various periodicals carried a short notice that Gratiana planned to publish a book (or booklet) about R. D. Blackmore's *Lorna Doone: A Romance of Exmoor*. She had 'made a study of the traditions and facts of the book', and planned to 'embody the results of her researches' in *The Forty Thieves of Exmoor; Or, The Doones of Badgworthy*.[86] She did indeed publish such a work in 1898—it was printed by Suckling & Co. of Garrick Street—but I have been unable to locate a copy.[87] Four years earlier, however, a short autobiographical story appeared in the *Auckland Star* entitled 'The Forty Thieves of Exmoor; or, The Doones of Badgworthy: The Author's Childhood in the Doone Valley, and Traditions Told Her'.[88] During the same year, she contributed a ballad, 'The Lady of Sevilla', to *Popular British Ballads: Ancient and Modern*.[89]

Gratiana's novella *The Witch of Withyford: A Story of Exmoor*, containing her own illustrations, was published by J. M. Dent & Co. in May 1896. In it, Nance Darvel, a gruesome woman who lives in a hovel, is intent on punishing a slight by destroying the life of the local squire. It is an uncanny tale of witchcraft, superstition child-theft and revenge, set in Gratiana's beloved Devonshire and told by an elderly servant of Withyford Grange. The *Pall Mall Gazette* described it as:

> 'The prettiest little book, in the daintiest binding, written in clear, delicate style and with only sufficient dialect to add piquancy to the narrative of the old servant of the Grange. The story breathes of the sweet Devon air, and is full of quaint folklore, and old world loyalty and simplicity, and the beauties of Tor and Combe are vividly described.'[90]

On 14 October 1896, Gratiana married Edward William Longworth Knocker at Brendon Church; she was thirty-nine years old at the time, and Edward was fifteen years her junior.[91] Edward was born in Dover on 3 September 1872, the eldest son of Edward Knocker (1805-1884) and Canadian born Jane Celia Bayly Longworth Dames (1840-1884).[92] Three days after their wedding, Gratiana and Edward sailed from Plymouth to Naples on R. M. S. *Ophir*, a vessel renowned for its opulent interiors that went on to serve as the royal yacht.[93] They spent the first two years of their marriage in Italy, where Gratiana painted a great deal,[94] returning to Millslade in 1898. On 1 August of that year, Mabilla Chanter married Edward Western, a schoolmaster,[95] and following her honeymoon she left Brendon and moved to her husband's home in Dunster. Gratiana and Edward settled down to life at Millslade with Katherine.

While Gratiana was living in Italy, Twiss & Son, the local publisher of *Wanderings in North Devon*, included one of her drawings, a sketch of Holy Trinity Church, in their *Illustrated Guide to Ilfracombe and North Devon* (see page opposite).[96] It is likely, given the number of travel books being produced at the time, that her drawings appeared in other guides to Ilfracombe.[97]

Church of St. Brendan in the village of Brendon.

Holy Trinity, by Gratiana Chanter, from *Illustrated Guide to Ilfracombe.*

In September 1901, *The Rainbow Garden and Other Stories*, a collection of eight 'graceful short stories for children',[98] illustrated by the author and written with 'a touch of pathos and mystery which will appeal to little folk',[99] was published by R. Brimley Johnson.[100] The critic for the *Westminster Review* wrote:

> 'Mr. Brimley Johnson has published a volume of delightful short stories... The tales have all the charm of fairy stories, and there is a thread of exquisite fancy running through them. Perhaps the melancholy note predominates too much in these little stories, which are apparently intended for children... But the writer of this volume of tales has certainly the gift of

touching the heart… though she writes in a strain of almost unbroken sadness.'[101]

It certainly is true that all of the stories have a melancholy air about them; in all but one, someone or something dies: children, flowers, bees, trees, a windmill… and even a year. But all of the tales in this extremely rare volume are enjoyable.

In 1806, Gratiana contributed one chapter to *The Book of Capri,* entitled 'Some Capri Flowers, and Where They Grow', which was written from her personal experiences of flower-hunting on the island, in the hope that her readers may 'linger long in Capri, and be happy amongst its flowers.'[102] Gratiana had visited Capri for the first time in 1896, when she and Edward stayed at the Hotel Paradiso; she went looking for holly to decorate their hotel room on Christmas Eve but had to make do with a bundle of myrtle and rosemary branches.[103]

In May 1908, Millslade, and the surrounding eleven acres of land, was sold at auction; the furnishings were sold a month later.[104] Katherine went to live with Mabilla and her husband in Minehead,[105] and Gratiana and Edward returned to Italy, where they remained for the rest of their lives; they lived in Pozzuoli in Naples, where Edward was employed by the Armstrong Works, then Rome, where he worked at the Department of the Commercial Counsellor at the British Embassy.[106]

Trebetherick, a tale of shipwrecks, wreckers, hidden treasure, abducted maidens, murder and other evil doings, was published in 1913 by Francesco Giannini & Figli of Naples. The story is told from the perspective of David Rounsevall of Trebetherick in the Parish of St. Enodoc, Cornwall, and begins the night he first hears ghostly Tregeagle howl during a ferocious storm. The reviewer for the *Birmingham Post* wrote:

'...the whole story is filled with the authentic atmosphere of the West country. It is not only that the "local colour" is plentiful and vivid; all the rest is in keeping. None but a West-country woman could have written it. And one cannot but feel that if her story is to enjoy its deserts it will have to become a classic of the Cornish book-stalls.'[107]

Trebetherick is a real place, thirty-five or so miles south of Morwenstow, and is located, as the story tells us, halfway 'between the Church of St. Enodoc and the hamlet of Polseth' (Polzeath). The church, famous for having been almost buried in sand until the second half of the nineteenth century, is the burial place of John Betjeman, who spent the last years of his life in the village of Trebetherick.[108] The Rounsevalls were also real, though whether or not they ever heard Tregeagle howl we shall never know.

When writing *Trebetherick*, Gratiana appears to have been inspired by actual events which took place in North Devon in 1842. She wrote in *Wanderings in North Devon*:

'In old days the evil practice of "wrecking" was carried on to a terrible extent all along the coast. One method of enticing vessels ashore, was to place lights in different spots along the cliffs. If the vessel was a foreigner, or without a pilot, it would often make for the light, the crew thinking it was placed there to guide them in.'[109]

She then described the wrecking of the *William Wilberforce* at Lee, a few miles from Ilfracombe, to demonstrate the villainy which wreckers were capable of. The legend goes that a donkey with a lantern tied to its tail was used to lure the ship onto the rocks; 'the action of the donkey on the beach caused the lantern to move up and down, just as a shiplight would by the action of the waves', leading those aboard the ship to believe they were heading for the safety of Ilfracombe harbour.[110]

The *William Wilberforce* was indeed wrecked at Lee during a heavy gale on 23 October 1842, at about seven o'clock in the evening, and all seven hands were lost.[111] Whether or not the vessel was lured onto the rocks by wreckers looking to loot her, with or without the aid of a donkey, William Huxtable, the Receiver General of Droits of Admiralty and sub-agent to Lloyds, was taking no chances; with the assistance of the Coast Guard Services, he stripped the ship of her sails and rigging immediately, then took possession of her cargo and removed her yards, topmasts, etc., the following day.[112]

Trebetherick was Gratiana's last published work. Edward died on 7 May 1933; he was sixty years old. Gratiana died the following year, on 24 November 1934, at the age of seventy-seven,[113] leaving her estate to her youngest sister, Charlotte Joyce. Gratiana and Edward were buried in the Campo Cestio, the non-Catholic cemetery, in Rome.[114]

Notes

1 For the date: birth certificate, district of Ilfracombe, registered 8 June 1857. Name listed as 'Graciana' (the spelling was altered to 'Gratiana' by 1881: see the *1881 England Census,* Norfolk, Kettlestone); she was also referred to as Grace. For the location: 'Girls That the Counties Are Proud Of', *The Girl's Realm Annual,* 1903, p. 831.

2 *Ferny Combes: A Ramble After Ferns in the Glens and Valleys of Devonshire,* was published by Lovell Reeve in 1856. Barnack is a village and civil parish in the Peterborough unitary authority of the ceremonial county of Cambridgeshire.

3 *Engand, Select Births and Christenings, 1538-1975.* Charlotte was baptised on 17 October 1828. There were seven children in all. The Kingsley's fifth child, Louisa Mary, died in infancy on 14 May 1824, four years before Charlotte's birth: *Stamford Mercury*, 21 May 1824, p. 3.

4 Lady Susan Chitty, *Charles Kingsley's Landscape: His Letters and Memories of His Life.* Newton Abbot: David & Charles, 1976, p. 8. Charles Kingsley served as curate from 1831, then rector from 1832 to 1836.

5 Gratiana Chanter, *Wanderings in North Devon: Being Records and Reminiscences in the Life of John Mill Chanter, M. A., Oxon, 51 Years Vicar of Ilfracombe.* Ilfracombe: Twiss & Son, 1887, p. 1.

6 Ibid., p. 3.

7 Ibid.

8 *Oxford University and City Herald*, 30 April 1836, p. 3.

9 Chanter, op. cit., p. 15.

10 Chanter, op. cit., p. 19.

11 Chitty, op. cit., p. 116.

12 Chanter, op. cit., p. 20.

13 *Bristol, England, Church of England Marriages and Banns, 1754-1938*, Clifton, St. Andrew, Gloucestershire.

14 Chanter, op. cit., pp. 15-16.

15 Ibid., p. 39.

16 Ibid. Pattens: wooden clogs or overshoes that elevate the foot to aid the wearer when walking on wet or muddy ground.

17 Ibid.

18 Ibid.

19 Chanter, op. cit., p. 38.

20 Ibid., p. 43.

21 *Lady's Newspaper and Pictorial Times*, 6 April 1850, p. 30.

22 *Western Times*, 14 June 1851, p. 4.

23 *North Devon Journal*, 17 March, p. 5.

24 *North Devon Journal*, 23 November 1854, p. 8.

25 *Italy, Find a Grave Index, 1800s-Present.*

26 *North Devon Journal*, 24 February 1859, p. 8.

27 *North Devon Journal*, 9 July 1863, p. 8.

28 Chanter, op. cit., pp. 33-34.

29 Ibid., p. 34.

30 *Ilfracombe Chronicle* included school examination results for 'light. heat, electricity' (physics), geography, geometry, and drawing, etc.

31 Chanter, op. cit., p. 40.

32 Ibid., p. 41.

33 Ibid., p. 40.

34 *Jack Frost and Betty Snow: With Other Tales for Wintry Nights and Rainy Days.* London: Griffith and Farran, 1858.

35 Chanter, op. cit., p. 49.

36 *North Devon Journal*, 18 September 1873, p. 8.

37 Ibid. Te octopus was taken to Rev. Lewis's aquarium and was 'alive and well' at the time of the news report.

38 'Girls That the Counties Are Proud Of', in *The Girl's Realm Annual*, 1903, p. 831.

39 Chanter, op. cit., p. 5.

40 Ibid., p. 6.

41 *The Girl's Realm Annual*, op., cit., p. 831.

42 Ibid.

43 Ibid.

44 Chanter, op. cit., p. 9.

45 *North Devon Journal*, 27 May 1875, p. 8 and *Ilfracombe Chronicle*, 12 May 1888, p. 5.

46 *Ilfracombe Chronicle*: 31 March 1883, p. 2 (Devon Artillery); 4 April 1885, p. 2 (Holy Trinity); 9 January 1886, p. 5 Girls' Schoolroom); 24 January 1874, p. 4 (town hall).

47 *Ilfracombe Chronicle*, 9 January 1886, p. 5.

48 Chanter, op. cit., p. 56.

49 Ibid., pp. 57-58.

50 Charles Edward Byles, *The Life and Letters of R. S. Hawker (Sometime Vicar of Morwenstow)*. London: John Lane. p. 617.

51 Ibid., p. 58.

52 Ibid., p. 59.

53 The auction was held on 25 June 1869 at the Golden Lion Hotel, Barnstaple. See *North Devon Journal*, 17 June 1869, p. 1.

54 Chanter, op. cit., p. 64.

55 There has been an inn on the site of the Fox and Goose since the 16th century. The one referred to by Gratiana burned down in 1892; the current Fox and Goose was built in 1894 (*The Historic Environment Record for Exmoor National Park*, MEM23816).

56 Chanter, op. cit., pp. 73-76.

57 Ibid., p. 77.

58 *UK, Apprentices Indentured in Merchant Navy, 1824-1910*. He was in Newcastle, New South Wales, Australia, when he deserted.

59 *Ilfracombe Chronicle*, 5 December 1974, p. 5.

60 *Ilfracombe Chronicle*, 23 January 1875, p. 5. He died on 1 August 1874 according to *England & Wales, National Probate Calendar (Index of Wills and Administrations), 1858-1995)*.

61 *Ilfracombe Chronicle*, 23 January 1875, p. 5.

62 Death certificate, district of Ilfracombe, county of Devon, registered 22 March 1882. Causes of death: chronic myelitis and lardaceous disease of the liver (now known as amyloidosis).

63 Byrom Bramwell, M. D., F. R. C. P. (Edin.). *Diseases of the Spinal Cord.* Second edition. Edinburgh: Young J. Pentland, 1884, p. 250.

64 John King, M. D., *The Causes, Symptoms, Diagnosis, Pathology and Treatment of Chronic Diseases.* Cincinnati: Moore, Wilstach & Baldwin, 1867, p. 188.

65 *Ilfracombe Chrinicle*, 11 August 1877, p. 5.

66 UK and Ireland, Find a Grave Index, 1300s-Current.

67 Death certificate.

68 *North Devon Journal*, 30 March 1882, p. 8.

69 Ibid.

70 Lily Chanter had married Rev. James F. Vallings on 20 August 1882; Mary, Mabilla, Gratiana, Katherine and Charlotte Joyce remained living with their father.

71 *Ilfracombe Chronicle*, 13 November 1886, p. 5.

72 *Ilfracombe Chronicle*, 11 December 1886, p. 5.

73 *North Devon Gazette*, 4 January 1887, p. 5.

74 *Ilfracombe Chronicle*, 2 April 1887, p. 3.

75 *Ilfracombe Chronicle*, 10 March 1888, p. 5.

76 Although Gratiana is listed as being the book's editor, the contents would appear to have been written by her, based on stories and information provided by her father. The second half of the book contains a selection of the vicar's sermons.

77 *North Devon Journal*, 22 September 1887, p. 2.

78 *England & Wales, National Probate Calendar (Index of Wills and Administrations), 1858-1995.*

79 *North Devon Journal*, 23 February 1893, p.8.

80 Ibid.

81 Ibid.

82 North Devon Journal, 25 October 1894, p. 3. The lych gate still exists and is a grade II listed building.

83 *North Devon Journal*, 23 February 1893, p.8. Mary Geraldine (known as Sister Geraldine, *1911 England Census*) and Charlotte Joyce (known as Sister Joyce, *1881 England Census*) were members of the Community of St. John Baptist, Clewer, an Anglican religious order of Augustinian nuns. Charlotte Joyce later became a sister of the Community of the Holy Name (*1911 England Census*).

84 *1891 England Census.*

85 *North Devon Journal*, 22 October 1891, p. 3.

86 *The Critic*, 17 December 1892, p. 349.

87 The work was advertised in the *Bookseller*, 6 May 1898, p. 77.

88 *Auckland Star*, 21 April 1894, p. 3. Republished in Gratiana Chanter, *The Witch of Withycombe and Other Stories*, Nezu Press, 2024.

89 Reginald Brimley Johnson, *Popular British Ballads: Ancient and Modern.* Volume 4. London: J. M. Dent & Co., 1894, pp. 152-154.

90 *Pall Mall Gazette*, 9 May 1896, p. 3.

91 *North Devon Journal*, 22 October 1896, p. 3 and *Devon, England, Church of England Marriages and Banns, 1754-1920.*

92 *Kentish Gazette*, 10 September 1872, p. 5. Edward was the eldest son of Edward and Jane Knocker. However, his father had been married twice before, with issue.

93 *UK and Ireland, Outward Passenger Lists, 1890-1960.*

94 *The Girl's Realm Annual*, op., cit., p. 831.

95 *Exeter and Plymouth Gazette*, 9 August 1898, p. 6.

96 No publication date, but the date included on a railway timetable within it suggests it was published in 1897.

97 As the names of the artists who provided illustrations for these tourist volumes are generally omitted, it would be necessary to compare Gratiana's known work with specific guide books.

98 *Bookseller*, 25 December 1901, p. 96.

99 *London Quarterly Review*, January 1902, p. 198.

100 *Westminster Gazette*, 21 September 1901, p. 8.

101 *Westminster Review*, November, 1901, pp. 593-594.

102 Harold E. Trower, *The Book of Capri*. Naples: Emil Brass, 1906, p. 301.

103 Ibid., p. 292.

104 *North Devon Journal*, 28 May 1908, p. 2.

105 *1911 England Census*.

106 Edward worked for The Armstrong Works, Pozzuoli-Cantiere, in 1918-1919, and he and Gratiana lived at Villa Suigi, Oriano, Pozzuoli, see *Over-Seas Club and Patriotic League: List of Subscribing Members, 1918-1919*, p. 105. p. 105 and *1919-1920*, p. 64. He worked at the British Embassy in Rome toward the end of his life and was awarded an O. B. E., see *The London Gazette*, 2 January 1933, p. 11. The couple lived at 22 Via Aipi in Rome at the time of their deaths, see *England & Wales, National Probate Calendar (Index of Wills and Administrations), 1858-1995*, 1933 and 1935.

107 *Birmingham Daily Post*, 20 May 1914, p. 4.

108 By the 1850s the local clergyman had to be lowered into the church via the skylight in the north transept to perform services (official list entry at Historic England, no. 1211902).

109 Chanter, op. cit., p. 69

110 Chanter, op. cit., pp. 69-70

111 *North Devon Journal*, 3 November 1842, p. 3, and *London Evening Standard*, 29 October 1842, p. 3.

112 *London Evening Standard*, 29 October 1842, p. 3. The figurehead of the William Wilberforce—an representation of the man himself—is now housed within the Cutty Sark's collection of Merchant Navy ships' figureheads, in Greenwich, London.

113 *England & Wales, National Probate Calendar (Index of Wills and Administrations), 1858-1995*, 1933 and 1935.

114 *Italy, Find a Grace Index, 1800s-Current.*

PROLOGUE

IT has come to me many a time while sitting in the dusk and watching the sparks fly upwards in the chimney, while the wind howled without and the waves thundered on the Bar, that I would write the story of Trebetherick.[1] Write of its living ones, of its loves, of its joys and sorrows, and may be of its dead, and of the winds and the sea which have ever been the fates of Trebetherick.

Royal saith, "Write it Cousin David: it will be a story indeed, better than any printed book."

But I am no scholar and gifted with little learning, and Royal hath ever thought too kindly of me, so have I hitherto been tardy in setting myself to the task, though Parson Trehern, when I was but a lad was greatly pleased with the hold I had on the pen, and indeed it was most surely through Parson Trehern that I first went to Bodmin School, and gathered there the little leaning which I endeavoured to keep close to me through the years which came after.

Being a cripple, I must needs be somewhat of a solitary lad, my brother Seth being ever otherwise, sturdy, lusty, and full of life, off all day long with the other lads of Polseth, ranging everywhere, over rock, cleeves, and downs.[2] But how could I keep up with him with my bent back and weak legs.

So it came to pass that I was mostly by myself, but making that I could of all that I heard or saw, creeping down to the edge

---

[1] Bar: a build up of sand where a river or harbour meets the open sea.

[2] Cleeve: a cliff, the steep side of a hill.

of the sea, listening to the sound of the wind through the rushes, or the cry of the birds on the shore; and for ever to the voice of the sea, which seemed calling, calling through everything else. And maybe through this same lonesomeness my thoughts they grew too full, for I would hear strange things on the sand-dunes and see strange forms in the clouds, while at night times when lying beside my brother Seth, faces of those I knew not would peer down upon me through the darkness, now coming nearer, and then again further away, making mouths at me and causing me such fear that I would lay hold of Seth in his sleep, crying loudly on him for help.

And so I must set all these strange fancies down, all that I saw or heard, on a Delabole slate which was over from roofing the cowshed.

I was so one day with my slate in the dusk when Parson Trehern came in to see my mother, he having ever shewn her much kindness since her great trouble came upon her, and it fell that his eye turned upon me where I sat in my corner pencil in hand.

"Martha," he said, "what is that lad doing there with his slate?" My mother gave a quick glance at me and turned to the parson answering him in a low voice, but I could hear the words she spake.

He's just as full of fancies," she said, "as a cornstack be full of straw, always putting down some nonsense or another on that old cracken slate of his. If it wasn't that he sets such store by it, I'd have thrown it out on the dung heap long before this," and she heaved a sigh, and looked again to where I sat.

Then Parson Trehern came over and took the slate from my hands and sat himself down on the settle to read by the light of the fire that which I had written, while I in my corner sat trembling near as much I do believe as the night when first I heard Tregeagle howl.[3] I watched him as he slowly read down my slate, and my heart beat as I watched, wondering in my mind to which part he might now have come; suddenly he gave a sharp look at me from over his spectacles at which I trembled the more, then taking them off he breathed heavily upon them, rubbing them well at the same time with the help of his red bandanna.

"Martha," he said, still cleaning his glasses the while, "you send that boy to school. He has been born with a pen in his hand, and, most surely, it is but the fair thing that he should be taught how to use it."

Now I had never seen my mother before so put out by Parson Trehern, but that she did not like his words that day I could see by the way she turned her head and made a clattering with the pans.

"Better by far," she answered back, "he'd been born with a silver spoon in his mouth, 'tis little he'll be doing in this world without it, I'm thinking; pen or no pen."

"Now that is just like you women," said Parson Trehern, "this lad is not only born with a pen in his had, but with brains in his head, and the two together my good Martha are worth more than a million of your grandmother's spoons."

Then they lowered their tones and talked together for some while, and I could no longer catch their words, so I crept away to my place in the attic to think over what I had heard, though at the time I made little of what they had spoken, my chief thought being that Parson Trehern had neither laughed at or chided me; with a great longing for my Delabole slate the while.

---

[3] Jan Tregeagle, the doomed spirit whose ghostly wails can be heard along the coast and across the moors of Cornwall on cold, dark, stormy nights.

And it was after this that I went to Bodmin School, though but for three short years, my mother and Uncle Joshua deeming it all that was necessary.

This much have I written about myself to show how it comes that I have so little clerkly knowledge, but if ever my story be finished and come to scholarly eyes, they will look kindly on its many errors, thinking maybe if I had bided longer at Bodmin School I might have done somewhat of that which good Parson Trehern foretold.

CHAPTER I

THE WORDS OF ANTHONY GUY AND HONOR HIGGS

Trebetherick, the home of the Rounsevalls, standeth half way up the steep hill between the Church of St. Enodoc and the hamlet of Polseth. From its upper windows when the tide be high you may watch the breakers leaping on the bar, for it faceth that way, and when the tides be low you may see the bare ribbed golden sands spread out, veined with blue runnels and alive with countless sea birds seeking their meat amongst the heaps of weed and refuse left behind. Near across to Stepper Point do they stretch on the other side, save for the narrow flow of water where the River Camel winds forth to meet the sea; and to my thinking they are ever a pleasant sight with the sunlight full upon them, and the white whirl of seabirds' wings, as blown foam or flakes of snow.

Trebetherick itself be an ancient place. For many and many a generation have the Rounsevalls lived and died within its walls. You may see their names in St. Enodoc churchyard where the stones show above the sand, and again in the churchyard beside the water over against Rock.

Yes, it be an old fashioned and ancient place Trebetherick, with gabled windows above and lattice below, the stonework about the same being of Cornish granite, and slated strongly on the roof with heavy Delabole slate. It stands with its back to the shelter of the hill, and its face towards the south, while to the westward, where the salt storms cut the keenest, stand a group of wind swept beeches covering it somewhat from the heaviest fall of the blast, at the same time giving shelter to the box edged pleasance where my mother kept her few bits of flowers. Behind are cowsheds with a yard for the cattle and the great granite drinking trough, not forgetting the mighty heap of mixen which was ever the pride and joy of the heart of Anthony Guy.[4]

Inside was the great kitchen where we mostly sat, with the parlour opening therefrom, where my mother kept her treasure of silver, the best china, and the old dish with the name "Richard Rounsevall" engraven thereon; also there was the family Bible wherein all the Christian names of the Rounsevalls for many generations were inscribed, with the births, deaths, and marriages of the same, which my mother set great store by. This room we rarely used save when we had visitors, such as Parson Trehern or Uncle Christian Clemoes of Padstow. Indeed it was a room set apart and in no ways to be treated commonly, nor did Seth and I ever dare enter it (saving on Sundays when we had on our newly blackened shoes) under the penalty of a clout on the head and many angry words from Honor Higgs, who looked on the parlour of Trebetherick as little short of the Holy of Holies. Indeed I have often heard her say that whenever she dreamed of heaven it was ever the parlour of Trebetherick she saw, with my mother's china in the cupboard and the family Bible laid out upon the table.

My father and Uncle Joshua were the masters of Trebetherick, but my father took to the sea. For it hath ever been so that one of each generation must leave all that he hath and cleave to the sea. They may bide at home for a space and be seemingly content, but the time will surely come when the call of it gets too strong for them, and out of Padstow harbour they will sail, some maybe for many a year, and others never to return.

---

[4] Mixen: a dunghill, mire.

It was so my father took to the sea like the rest. Not even his young wife nor the bright lad Seth could keep him back from it. The call had come and he must follow it, as Rounsevalls had done before him and Rounsevalls will again. And it was so that Uncle Joshua looked after the farm, till he terrible time came which left my mother a widow, and me with my weak back and crooked legs to help out the sorrow of it.

Now all that I know concerning that which befell before my father's death, or of that terrible time when the sea washed him up at my mother's feet on Polseth Strand, have I heard alone from Honor Higgs and Anthony Guy, my mother never speaking of her trouble, but keeping it close to herself, until it grew so large within her it could but gaze out of her eyes, even as a dead face out of a window.[5] All who looked could see it, poor soul, though she reckoned she'd locked the door.

Honor Higgs and Anthony Guy, were maid and man to Trebetherick, they were so when I was born, so knew well my mother's trouble. Never did they speak of that same time to me, but only with each other when the work was over, and mostly did it seem to be upon their minds when the wind blew high without.

I mind well one night when it happened my mother had gone to visit the Popes of Pentire Glaze, that they sat talking in low tones over the fire, while I crouched low by the side of Honor watching the light among the logs, and shivering at that which they spake.[6]

Anthony Guy was smoking his long pipe of clay in the corner of the settle, his face and wrinkled throat showed red in the glow of

[5] Strand: shore, beach.

[6] Mind: remember.

the fire. Honor was knitting a long blue stocking and her needles chirped perpetually as a cricket behind the wainscot. The wind was howling round the house and roaring in the chimney. The corners of the room showed black and full of mystery, while the white face of the clock stared at me out of the gloom. I crept close to Honor Higgs and took hold of her thick stuff dress, for there was comfort in the touch of it. Then Anthony Guy blew a cloud of smoke from his mouth, which the draught caught hold of and whirled up the chimney. " 'Tis roughish night for the missus to be out," he said in his slow drawling tones, "the waters coming down fit to drown a body, and the wind blowing properly cruel."

"Iss fie! Iss fie! you'm right," answered Honor bending forward to pick up a stitch by the light of the fire.[7] "Her standeth a good chance to be blown into say, crossing Pentire Glaze such a night as this here."[8]

Anthony Guy cleared his throat loudly, then sat for a while silent, puffing hard at his pipe which seemed ever as oil to his speech, making it come the easier.

"May be," he said at length, "there be worse things about such a night as this than wind and water, aye worse things I'd say Honor Higgs, and not so natural mind you—and not so natural."

Honor started and dropped her knitting in her lap. "Man alive! what do 'e mane?" she cried, and looked quickly over her shoulder and round to the darkened corners of the room, till her eyes met the white face of the clock peering down at her through the darkness; and I heard her give a catch to her breath that was almost like a

---

[7] Iss fie: lit. 'yes faith'. Used as an assertion or quasi-oath, meaning 'yes, by my faith', 'yes, verily' or 'yes, truly'.

[8] Say: sea.

cry. "Oh Lord! Anthony Guy," she cried, "what be telling of![9] Hold your noise do if you've nought else to say."

But Anthony Guy seemingly did not hear, but cleared his throat again and spat into the fire, a way he had when showing a desire to talk.

"Now, Honor Higgs," he said dropping his voice to a solemn tone, and marking off what he said the while on his fingers. "You know every bit as well as I do, that this here be the very sort of night for to hear the call of Tregeagle."

"Lord!" cried Honor with a gasp, "and if it be what need be there to tell of it."

The wind screamed round the house and shook with an angry hand at the shutters. A puff of it came down the chimney sending the smoke inwards and setting my eyes watering with the fumes of it. I thought of my mother battling round Pentire Glaze with the raging sea below, and I clung the tighter to the folds of Honor's gown, gazing hard into the glow of wood and coals, trying with all my strength to forget the darkened room behind and the rain and wind without. Then Anthony Guy went on again in his slow and heavy tones. " 'Twas just such a night as this here," he cried, "as Tregeagle *did* call, and the master was washed up a corpse on Polseth Strand for all the folk to see."

Honor rocked herself to and fro while the wind moaned round the house and the rain drove against the window pane.

"Aye," said Anthony Guy again taking his pipe from his mouth as I had seen him do when a funeral was passing by, "washed up a corpse he was for all the folk to see."

" 'Tis truth, 'tis truth," cried Honor flinging her apron over her

[9] What be telling of: what are you talking about.

head, while she rocked her body to and fro. " 'Tis truth sure enough! Tregeagle has ever brought trouble to this house: and the poor child be a living witness of it with his rounded back and the weak legs of him."

Now I ever believe that Honor Higgs must have thought that I had fallen asleep, or that she was too much taken up with her thoughts, to take any account of my presence, for she had a good heart and ever a kindly pity for my weakness in spite of her rough ways. But child as I was I felt at that moment the full shame of her words, and crouching the lower beside her chair I clenched my small hands tight to prevent calling out with the pain of them. And never to my dying day shall I forget the words of Anthony Guy and Honor Higgs as they sat talking that night over the kitchen fire of Trebetherick, nor the nameless horror which the name of Tregeagle for ever after had for me. For whenever the wind would rise and the voice of it shrieked in the chimney, or howled through the beech trees without, I would lie shuddering in my bed fearing each moment to hear the call of the evil one, which had brought such great sorrow to the home and crippled me from my cradle. Indeed it was but a few months after that night of which I have spoken, that we, one and all, of Trebetherick did hear that self same call, and knew the full meaning and horror of it.

CHAPTER II
THE HOWL OF TREGEAGLE

'TWAS the month of October I mind, and near about the end of it, when the winds and the sea which have ever been the fates of Trebetherick, brought that ashore that boded no good to the place.

'Tis an ill wind, most surely! which bloweth no blessing, but it would take a cleverer man than the Lord ever thought fit to make me, to see aught but ill in that which came with the blast and roar of that night's tempest.

It is often but little things of small account which lead up to great ones, and so that day which was to bring so much to us all opened with small beginnings, but all of which stand out sharp and clear in my sight and hearing as though they happened but yesterday.

I was home from Bodmin School for a space and my mother had sent me that day as far as Padstow Town with my Uncle Joshua to do a bit of shopping. We rode by way of the sand hills to Rock, a matter of a mile or so, I on the grey pony and my uncle on the mare.

We left the horses in old Miss Mably's linhay, and crossed by way of the ferry boat which plies from Rock to Padstow, and then after doing my mother's biddings, we went on a visit to my Uncle Christian Clemoes, the shipbuilder.[10] There, Uncle Joshua sat awhile and smoked a pipe, while my cousin Royal and I went into the apple orchard behind the house to play. We stayed some time there, busy picking up the rosy apples in heaps against the time they should be wanted for the cider-press, when a call from

---

[10] Linhay: a type of open-fronted farm building.

my Uncle Joshua warned me it was time to go. As I bid Royal goodbye at the door she held something out to me wrapped up in a dock leaf and tied tightly about with string.

"There be three Cornish gillyflowers for you, cousin David," she said, "at least there be one for you and *two* for Seth." I remember well how my Uncle Christian laughed at her words, and the way she stood in the doorway with her finger to her lips as we walked away. Ah! sweet cousin Royal, so it was ever—*two* for Seth.

It was blowing up for a storm as we came homeward across the sand hills. The wind came in spiteful gusts catching the sands upwards in whirls and eddies, forcing us to keep our heads down and at times our eyes shut tight against it; the path between the rushes showing but dimly in the grey of the twilight, we had to trust to our beasts to guide us free of the rabbit holes.

Black clouds, torn and twisted, moved heavily before the coming gale casting shadows as they went. The Doom-bar moaned, the sea heaved in sullen leaden rolls, while the breakers leaped as angry beasts round Pentire Head and Gallard, both inky blue against the smeared crimson of the sky.

"Sure there'll be a storm before morning," said Uncle Joshua, "and a pretty stiff one too, or I don't know the signs. I pity they as gets near Pentire Head this night. The Lord save them, for it's little chance they'll have to save themselves. Keep your hat tight, lad, and your eyes open, and go softly for the rabbit holes."

I mind I was mighty glad to get in that night to the warmth and glow of the fire, with the scent and sound of mushrooms frying in the pan, and the clatter of coming supper which Honor Higgs was preparing.

I mind my mother was out that night, for she had gone to visit Mistress Trewint of Pentire Farm, with whom she had a friendship, and so as the supper was ready, and our appetites somewhat keen with our ride across the sand hills, it came that we sat down without her, while the wind howled without, and the fire of drift-wood upon the hearth glowed and crackled within.

We were well forward with our meal, and I remember thinking the taste of the mushrooms mighty fine, and Seth and I wishing that Honor had been more generous in the fry of them, when a sound came on the wings of the wind which made us drop our knives and catch our breath sharp, freezing the blood in our veins and keeping us still in our places as folks turned to stone.

'Twas a piercing long-drawn scream which seemed to have no end to it, whirling along on the wings of the blast, it came nearer and nearer, crying, moaning, calling, till the pain of it seemed past the bearing.

Then did it whimper low and soft as a human creature in trouble, and then break forth again in shrill and piercing cries as one in fiendish torment, and ever the wind blew with it stronger and stronger, till it seemed a raging battle between the tortured thing and the storm. Then as though gathering all its strength together the wind rose with one mighty effort, roaring and thundering round old Trebetherick, setting it shaking where it stood. Then sudden it seemed to leave its hold on us, dragging the evil thing along with it, weeping and moaning as it went, onwards across the uplands into the blackness of the night.

The last faint wail of the evil thing had scarce died away in the darkness, and we were still seated about the table, scarce daring to draw a breath in fear that the dreadsome cry might come back with the blow of the blast, when the door burst open, and with a rush of cold air and the smell of the storm behind her, my mother stood before us, the loose black cloak she wore dripping and heavy with rain. Her face was ashen white as that of the dead and her great eyes mazed and wild.[11] She stood for a minute or so with her hand upon the door nob, the wind that came in with her setting the tallow dip guttering upon the table.

"You have heard it," she cried, "you have heard it. My God! It is Tregeagle."

Then she dropped where she stood as a stone upon the floor, and lay there as one who was dead.

---

[11] Mazed: mad.

CHAPTER III

HELL'S BAY

THAT troubles rarely come alone, is a true saying, also that many joys may be gathered in one bunch again being truth, one may tell that in the long run the things in this world are dealt fairly to us.

But it was more of the first sort which was blown to us of Trebetherick that stormy night of October, though I do not forget that the other kind came to us later, for which the Lord be thanked.

My poor mother was in a sad way for some hours after her fall and it was some while before she clearly got her senses back, and was able to rise up and move about the kitchen. Then did she seem possessed by one strong thought, and she set herself and all in the house straightway to carry out the same.

It was Anthony Guy she sent to fetch the great coil of rope which hung on a peg in the passage, also him she told to fix a new rush light in the horn lantern, while Honor she sent upstairs for the blankets, bidding her set them before the fire against they were needed, while she herself set to work filling a lidded basket full of cordials, meats and restoratives.

"They will be wanted," she said in a low voice to herself, "most surely wanted to-night."

All did as she bid them without hesitation, or thought of saying her nay. Tregeagle had called that night, and all knew that ever meant something terrible to the house of Trebetherick, my poor mother most of all.

Uncle Joshua was sitting by the fire smoking his pipe, and though he seemed to be taking but little notice of that which was going on, I could see like the rest of us he was waiting for something more.

Now it was even as Honor Higgs was spreading the blankets to the blaze, and my mother was yet busy with her basket, that a sound came up the combe which set us all on our feet and sent my uncle and Anthony Guy to the door.[12]

A heavy dull sound it was, which seemed to break far away to seaward, the like of which I had never heard before, but was no new thing to my uncle or Anthony Guy. They both went hastily out to the gate leaving the door open behind them, letting in the cold sea air and the smell of the night; and again the dull sound broke, and seemed to roll towards us.

'Tis a ship in distress, sure enough, my Uncle Joshua said as he came in and shut the door behind him. "You're ready none too soon Martha, woman, she's making for Hell's Bay or the Doombar by the sound of her. May the Lord have mercy on them."

My mother pinned a black shawl about her head, and put on a warm cloak, telling Honor the while to see to the fire and keep all in readiness for those whom the Lord might think fit to save that night. She saw that Uncle Joshua took the ropes and a bundle of warm things along with him, sending Anthony Guy before with a lantern, while she took up her basket and followed them into the night.

It was after they had gone that Seth and I sat still on the settle watching Honor as she turned the blankets, and put away the supper things. And I mind seeing that there were still some mushrooms left upon Seth's plate, which knowing his great liking for those things I greatly wondered at, though now I surely know how great his fear must have been at the time of Tregeagle's call: and 'tis ever the sight and scent of those things which brings back to me clearer

[12] Combe: a steep, short valley running up from the sea.

than aught else I know (saving it be the roar of the westerly gale in the chimney) the doings of that dreadsome night, when first I heard Tregeagle call.

'Twas well enough for us so long as the homely sound of Honor's pattens clacked back and fore across the floor, but when she say down in her chair before the fire, and her head began to nod with the heaviness of sleep which overcame her, and there were only the sounds of the night outside, and the squeaking of rats behind the wainscot, then did I and my brother Seth begin to feel terribly lonesome, and crept the closer to each other for company.[13]

And ever and again there came to our ears the solemn booming of the guns from the ship in grievous trouble.

So did we sit that whole night through while sleep never came to our eyes, in the fear that every moment the door might open and something terrible come through to be laid in the blankets still warming before the fire.

So the night went by, neither Seth or I daring the while so much as to peep round the further corner of the settle to the place where the window was, 'till it came to us of a sudden that a new light was filling the room, cold and pale, but nought else but the dawn of another day.

Then Honor gave a mighty yawn, and roused herself up, putting fresh fuel upon the fire, which gave out a cheerful crackle as she did so.

"The day be here at last," she cried, "Lord what can they be doing of down to say all this long while.[14] Here I reckon as you

---

[13] Pattens: wooden clogs or overshoes that elevate the foot to aid the wearer when walking on wet or muddy ground.

[14] Down to say: down by the sea.

children will be wanting a glass of milk and a slice of cake," and so did she bustle away to the dairy to get the same.

At the sound of Honor's homely voice, things seemed more natural, and, as the light grew stronger, the familiar things about us showed out more plainly, the sight of them sending the night away, and its fears along with it. And it was after a glass of milk, and a goodly slice of my mother's saffron cake, that we at length found courage to slip from the settle and stretch our legs a bit.

It was then that the restlessness which overtakes boys possessed us, so that we opened the door and went out to the gate to see if we could hear aught of that which was happening out beyond. We felt it a good thing to be breathing the salt air in through our nostrils with the taste of the sea in our mouths.

The rain has ceased and the wind had somewhat abated, but still it was blowing hard enough when we opened the gate, and met the full force of the blast, to make it a difficult matter for slight lads like ourselves to stand up against it. We could see the grey breakers below dashing up on Granaway Strand, with the foam bells drifting inland as flights of wind-swept sea birds, and ever the roar of the sea and the rush of the blast were filling our ears. And with the sound of it, a longing came over us both to see for ourselves, and know what was happening down there by the sea. Fearing that Honor, if she knew of our intention, would tell us to bide in the house, we made off as we were, Seth leading the way down the steep lane which leads to Granaway Strand.

'Twas crossing Granaway Strand that we found the wind almost too much for us. I was for turning back, but Seth would not hear of it, though the drive and the smart of the sand in our eyes made us near cry with the pain of it. But gaining the low down where the Granaway rocks begin, our going became somewhat easier, for we got under the storm a bit, and there it was we sat down 'neath the shelter of some tamerisk bushes to get our breath and clear out our eyes.

'Twas then that we saw one John Trewhit of Polseth crossing the strand, and sitting close to our shelter till he came up with us, we asked him for news of the wreck.

John Trewhit stared down upon us where we crouched together beneath the tamerisk. "Now what be you two a doing of here," he said, "you'll be blowed into say sure enough. Best go home to once and bide long with Honor, or you'll be blowed into say."[15]

"Bide long with Honor," cried Seth tossing his curls, "not very like! we've come so far, and us baint going back, John Trewhit."[16]

So onward we went across the downs keeping the land-ward side of John, who being the stoutest man in Polseth it bettered us much to travel that way. And it was after we had turned the corner where the rocks reach out of Hell's Bay that we came full upon the little crowd who were watching the ship that was doomed.

But I could give no thought to the folk, nor could I tell who was there. I could give no eyes to aught but the grey drift above, the heaving boiling sea below, and that which was in the midst of it.

She was almost within a stone's throw of us, being driven nearer every moment. The heavy seas were breaking over her, and all her masts had gone save one, and to that a man was clinging. No other living thing was aboard, for the sea had claimed them all. 'Twas a rising tide, so that the cruel current was dragging her inch by inch towards the sharpest teeth of Granaway rocks, into the very mouth of Hell's Bay. She plunged and writhed like a human

---

[15] Best go home to once and bide long: Best go home at once and stay.

[16] Baint: ain't.

creature in pain, a helpless thing at the mercy of the cruel sea. So did the breakers leap and roar above her, dragging her nearer and nearer to her end.

Then did I see an awful thing which I shall ne'er forget unto my dying day. The swinging, swaying mast with the poor creature clinging to it snapped sharply in two, and he who was clutching it dropped as a stone into the surging, boiling sea, and none set eyes on him again.

The Polseth folks had done all they could to get ropes across the ship, but the wind had been too heavy for them to carry, so they could do nought but bide there watching and waiting hour after hour for the end.

And there the vessel stayed writhing and straining in her death agony. Then did a great sea lift her up, and, bringing her swiftly onwards, crash her down on the rocks so that she split clean in two before our eyes, and there indeed did she stay for a while, her two halves jammed tight between the black teeth of the rocks.

Then began a cruel sport, the great waves tearing and mangling at her till the planking of her deck stood upon end and stayed there, never would I have believed the sea had such power unless I had seen it for myself. It tore her cargo from her till the sea around was strewn with floating kegs, strange foreign golden fruits and all sorts, and it was then that the Polseth folk showed most plainly the blood that was in them, and went running along the shore.

And it was then for the first time that I looked about to see who was amongst them. Parson Trehern was there with his hat tied under his chin by the help of his red bandanna, the Popes from Pentire Glaze and most of the men indeed from Polseth, but I did not see my mother, and much I wondered where she might be.

CHAPTER IV
POLSETH STRAND

NOW of the rest of that morning's doings, and of all that which befell on Polseth Strand, can I only speak from hearsay, Parson Trehern having spoken somewhat sharply to Seth and myself, bidding us get on our homeward way as quickly as we might, such a scene as the present being no fit place for boys like ourselves.

But it seems that after we left Parson Trehern he questioned the folks as to who had last seen my mother, and it was John Trewhit who told him that he had caught sight of her but a short while agone, hurrying backwards across the cliffs in the direction of Polseth Strand.

And my Uncle Joshua knowing of the night's work and how it had gone with my mother, spoke of the same to Parson Trehern, so it came that together with John Trewhit they made all haste the could along the path across the downs which they surmised she had taken.

Below them lay Hell's Bay, seething and churning like a boiling cauldron, out of which, the Padstow seamen will tell you, no ship comes alive, while across the restless spread of waters, through the grey drift from the sea, loomed the mighty headland of Pentire.

They kept along the path, the wind driving them forward, the foam bells flying past them as snowflakes before the blast, till they came where the path drops downward to the yellow level of the strand. Sure it was here that they found my mother.

She was standing waist deep in the water with her arms stretched out before her, and there, midst the heaving troughs of the waves, being ever tossed hither and thither, swung the black form of a boat; one moment it seemed near a shore, but the next the rough waves caught it again in their hold, dragging it far out of reach. Now and again did my mother give out a loud cry for help, but she gave no thought to herself but seemingly only to the black thing heaving and tossing beyond, and ever as it left her did she take a deeper step, till those who saw her feared every moment the waves would have her in their hold and drag her out to sea.

It took Parson Trehern but a short time to get along side of her, and gripping her arm he dragged her back from the sea.

"Go back, Martha," he said sternly, "go back at once from the sea, and bide there."

She stared at him in a dazed way, and struggled in his hold, pointing the while to the boat still spinning and tossing in the grey troughs of the sea.

"Save them! save them Parson!" she cried wildly, and seemed as one demented, crying, and pointing ever to the tossing thing in the waves.

Then my Uncle Joshua, together with John Trewhit, waded out up to their armpits, indeed as near as they dared to that which the sea had hold of; so close did it come to them once that John he had his hand on it, but the tide dragged it back again a long ways beyond their reach.

Then came a mighty sea thundering and swelling along which carried them off their feet, but brought the boat along side of them, both gripped at it tight, and with it were flung up high on Polseth Strand not loosing their hold the while. It was then that Parson Trehern and my mother came to their help, and quickly before the seas could reach them again, they had dragged that which they had hold of well up upon the beach.

It took my Uncle Joshua and John Trewhit some little time to recover themselves after that which they had gone through, for they were badly bruised and half drowned by the way the sea had treated them. Parson Trehern was giving them a hand, his first thought being for a nasty cut which John had got in the head, when sudden my mother uttered a cry, and with one accord they turned to her where she stood. She held in her hand a heavy bit of tarpauling, which seemingly, when they landed the boat, was all she had held. But beneath it, strapped firmly to the bottom, there lay now before their eyes, two of the loveliest children the sun ever shone on, but white as the dead, and indeed as dead they deemed them.

But my mother, at the sight, hushed her wild cries and with the help of Parson Trehern quickly set about cutting the stout cords which bound them. Then did they take off the sodden sea-men's coats in which they were wrapped, rolling the children up in the blankets which Uncle Joshua had brought along with him. "Dead or alive," my mother said, "we will take them home to Trebetherick."

So did they carry the little burdens up along the Polseth road and so did they lay them in front of the full blaze of the fire at Trebetherick, my mother and Honor Higgs the while doing all in their power to bring them back to life, while Seth and I watched them with wide open eyes, knowing now for whom Honor Higgs had warmed the blankets.

And there they lay before the fire as figures carved in marble over a tomb, a man child and a little maid, they seemed near about the age of Seth and me, with hair as black as ripened sloans, and so near alike in features you scarce could tell the difference.[17]

[17] Sloans: Sloe berries, from the *Prunus spinosa.*

Life first came back to the boy, and then the red showed in the lips of the little maid, my mother giving a cry of joy as she saw it, for most surely her care and the warmth of the fire were doing their work. Then did the boy open his great eyes, dark as wells, and stare up at Honor Higgs.

"He'll do, he'll do! Honor," said Parson Trehern rubbing his hands, "that boy's not born to be drowned I reckon, anyway not yet awhile."

"Pray the Lord he aint born to be hanged,' said Honor with a grunt.

Then did the little maid open her eyes and fix them straight on the parson's kindly face, as he bent over her, nor did she loose her gaze on him for some few minutes.

"Sure she's taken a fancy to you Parson," said Honor with a laugh.

"Poor little maid," said the parson, gently putting back the damp hair which clung about her brow. "Poor little maid, cast upon a rough shore, maybe she is wondering what strange folk she has fallen among."

"Strange or no," said Honor with another grunt, "if it wasn't for they, her wouldn't be alive this minute."

Then did a curious thing happen, which seems to me now as an omen of much which came after.

My mother was still at work upon the boy, rubbing him gently now here and now there, when sudden he turned and caught her hand that held him, tightly between his teeth so that my mother cried out with the pain of it, nor would he let go of her until Parson had stooped down and forced him to it. The blood from my mother's hand dropped on the snowy whiteness of his breast, and stayed there showing crimson in the firelight.

"Well, well," said Parson Trehern, "that small Viper is most assuredly alive and kicking, but the one the holy Paul warmed at the fire showed more gratitude than this small heathen, I'm thinking. Have a care Martha woman and don't let him get a second bite at you."

"Viper sure enough," cried Honor Higgs, "to bite the very hand as dragged un from the say, and near got drowned themselves in the doing of it. Better fit to have left un where he was, the little varmint. Mark my words, as no good will come of this here night's doings." And I thought she handled him somewhat roughly as she rolled him in the blanket before carrying him to mine and Seth's bed, we sleeping on a mattress on the floor of my mother's room that night.

And so it was that the two strange children came to bide with us at Trebetherick, for no other living soul was washed ashore to tell us who they were or whence they came. They spoke between themselves a strange language of their own, which Parson Trehern did say was either of Spain or Italy, being more like unto the Latin than aught else he knew. The boy ever spoke of the little maid as Vita, while he answered her when she called him by the name Diavolo, which Parson Trehern said was curiously near to the Latin name for the Evil One. My mother not liking this, said we must find some other good sounding Christian name whereby we might call him; but Honor Higgs who was by at the time, said the name was his own, and he'd best keep it! and keep it he did in more ways than one, as the story will show.

CHAPTER V

THE WAYS OF THE CHILDREN

NOW of the next five or six years it is but little that I have to write, saving those things which in the boy do go to make the man. For as we begin life, there is little doubt so do most of us go on with it, whether it be as a dreamer, or those who fight, or as good-for-naughts, or they of great worth. I do not say that we stay in the same place, but as the dreams or fighting are in us to start with, so be the evil and the good, and as time goes on they strengthen or weaken as the case may be, but there is ever some of the old leaven in us to the end.

Now the two strange children, Vita and Volo as we had got to call them, though at first the foreign names came clumsily to our lips, had been nigh four years at Trebetherick. They had near dropped their foreign talk, and picked up our own with great quickness. The maid was then about twelve years of age, and the boy as far as could be told, just going into his fourteenth. They were a handsome pair, and as wild and daring as a gale of wind in March, my mother at times scarce knowing how to manage them. Vita when she was crossed, would sit by the hour by herself with her face as dark and lowering as a November sky. But Volo would fling himself into a terrible rage, rolling on the ground and biting the dust as one possessed, till my mother could do naught else but send for Parson Trehern, he being the only one at such times who could in any way quiet him. Parson said he had been taught to fear the ministers in the country that he came from, and that it was fear which made Volo stop short in the midst of one of his rages when he saw the parson coming, and creep away and hide himself amid the cornstacks.

I mind it was just about this time, that one fine day my mother sent us all off cockling to Rock. We were to meet Royal Clemoes there, and bring her back for the night.

It was a lovely summer day, and we started off in high spirits with our oldest breeches on, and a goodly store of bags to hold the cockles. My legs were a bit stronger then, and I could keep fairly up with the rest, but I could never jump or run as Seth and Volo could, nor even as Vita.

We went past St. Enodoc's church, by way of the sand dunes to Rock. The grey rushes were scarce lifted by the breeze, sweet scents filled the air from the briar brakes and thickets of flowering privet.[18] The rabbits scurried away from our path, seeking their shady burrows, while the larks sang overhead. Below, to our right, stretched the golden sands, for the tide was low, with only the thin, blue, twisting line of the river Camel flowing through them, with patches of water here and there on the sand to show where the sea had been.

'Twas at Granny Mably's cottage that we at length met Royal Clemoes, in a pink cotton frock and bonnet, looking as fresh as day, and beautiful as she always must. Yes! beautiful she was surely! with her dancing eyes and sunshiney hair, and that laughing mouth of hers—and then her ways. Ah! her ways! Why I have heard even Honor Higgs declare that she had such ways with her as would turn sour cream sweet; and as to scolding her when she fell into any mischief, Honor said, "no human critter could do it," no not even when Royal took the cream off a newly scalded pan would Honor say a word to her, when to Seth or me it would have been a clout on the head, or a hoist with the help of a broom handle.

---

18 Brake: thicket.

I mind her that day as we left Granny Mably's, how she stepped across the road with her pretty bare feet, lifting them daintily up to avoid the rough stones, and then went flying onwards across the sands with Seth and Volo after her, sure there was no prettier sight to be seen. She minded me of a summer butterfly fluttering over the privet brakes on the burrows.

"Come my way!" cried Seth, "Come my way!" called Volo. But she only flew on the faster, laughing as she went.

It was some time we stayed out on the cockle-ridge, till our bags grew heavy, and my back beginning to ache with so much stooping and scraping, which is ever a necessity with this work, I left them to rest awhile on the dry sands under the shade of the dunes, where I could watch them as they picked.

Now I mind that Seth had left his bag on the mud, and was busy in helping Royal to fill hers, when I noticed that Volo had dropped behind and was picking his cockles close to where Seth's bag lay. I saw him take up Seth's bag bending low over it. but owing to his back being turned upon me I could not see clearly what he was about, but I reckoned that he was just looking to see how near Seth had filled it. Then as far as I saw he dropped it again on the mud, and went on and joined the others.

Now it was ever our way after cockling was over to empty our bags on the sand and to count out how many we had gathered, and childlike all were eager to carry the largest lot home to my mother. And so it was this day when they had got together all they wanted, that they came running back to where I sat, Seth carrying Royal's bag as well as his own, for it was heavy.

"Let's count them now," shouted Seth, flinging both bags as he spoke upon the sand, and himself beside them. Then taking up Royal's he emptied them out in a heap, while we all gathered round to watch the counting. She had a goodly lot, and I mind how she laughed and clapped her hands as the numbers began to go up, and how sure she was that her bag held more than any.

"Now Seth yours!" she cried when at length he came to the last. "Yours, yours, sure I don't believe that you've got more than me."

Seth stretched back for his bag which was laying behind him and as the full weight of it came upon his wrist, he gave a start and looked at it. The red flush showed on his face and an angry look in his eyes.

"Who's been meddling with my cockles?" he shouted. "Taint more than half full. I filled it brimming over, Royal knows I did."

Volo laughed a sneering laugh, "that's a fine tale," he said. "You're no good to the cockling, why just look at my bag. I've near got the double of yours," and he held up his bag as he spoke for all to see, and sure the cockles were bursting out through the noose at the top, so that he scarce could close the bag.

Seth flushed crimson as he saw it. "You thief!," he shouted springing to his feet. "You thief, you've been steeling mine, that's what you've been doing."

I had never seen Seth so moved before, for as a rule he was a slow lad to rouse. But this business of the cockles was a serious matter to us, and to carry home a half filled bag, when he had worked all day at the filling, proved too much for his temper. He stood there quivering with rage, both hands tightly clenched, staring angrily at Volo, while Volo, still with his sneering smile upon his face, shuffling first one bare foot and then the other in the sand, stood opposite to him, swinging the cockles slowly to and fro by the string the while.

Then did a curious change come over Volo's face, and he let the bag he held fall gently to the ground, and with the spring of a cat he had leaped upon Seth, while the next thing I saw Seth sick and reeling and Vita with her white teeth firm in Volo's wrist.

Volo gave a scream of pain, dropping the knife he held. Quick as lightning Vita swooped down upon it, flinging it far away into a sandy pool beyond.

Poor Seth sank faint upon the sand, the red blood slowly staining his white shirt where Volo had struck him. We were only children, and an awful fear came over us at the sight of it, with a terrible feeling of helplessness.

Royal stood there pale and trembling, clasping and unclasping her hands. Volo looked scared, Vita seemingly was the only one who kept her wits. She went to a pool and dipping her handkerchief in it, quick as light she was back again, bathing Seth's face and hands. Next she loosed his shirt, slipping it off his shoulders, and there was the cruel cut which Volo had given him bleeding terribly, making the poor lad faint with the pain of it.

Vita turned white at the sight, but went on steadily with her work. Taking her wet handkerchief she bound it firmly about his arm, bidding me help her with the tying of it. And after that it was to Vita and Vita alone that we all looked for help.

"We'd best get back to Granny Mably's as fast as we can," she said. "Maybe she'll give Seth some cordial and tell us what to do."

Vita and I helped Seth along, while Volo slunk behind, Royal carrying the cockles which had caused so much trouble, and crying softly the while. We had not far to go, and thankful we were when we got Seth safely inside Granny Mably's door.

Now it was after this affair of the cockles that Parson Trehern persuaded my mother to send Volo to my Uncle Christian Clemoes to learn the ship-building, thinking maybe he would have a firmer hand over him and the work might keep him from mischief.

It was the time of Padstow Revel, and not long after Volo had left Trebetherick, that we all went over for the day to my Uncle Christian Clemoes, Honor Higgs and Anthony Guy coming with us, my mother with Uncle Joshua biding home to look after the farm.[19]

My Uncle Christian's house looked out upon the Quay. From the parlour window you could see the folks pass up and down, the sailors grouped about or sitting on the walls, and the tall masts of the ships which lay in the harbour. And it was close outside my uncle's house that the best of the fair was to be seen, with its gaily coloured booths laden with such things as delight the eyes and hearts of children. Also near by were the shows where the giant and dwarf might be viewed, with the fat woman whose dimensions were ever a terror to me. Then there was the donkey who fired a loaded gun, along with the dog who walked a rope, and the folk who stood on their heads and walked on their hands, and ever a goodly show of cheap-jacks selling their different wares, making more noise with their shouting than all the rest of the folk put together.[20]

But first before reviewing the revel did we sit down to a mighty dinner, such as cannot be eaten anywhere save at my Uncle Christian Clemoes'; for it was cooked and set out by Sarah Richards, own sister to Honor Higgs, and being a widow woman without chick or chiel she was able to set her whole mind to it.[21] No other, you may depend, could make a pasty so tasty as Sarah Richards, or had so artful a twist in the baking of scrumps.[22]

---

[19] Revel: annual parish fair.

[20] Cheap-jacks: a peddler, often itinerant, of cheap and inferior goods.

[21] Chiel: child.

[22] Scrumps: apples.

It was after we had done full justice to all upon the table, and Honor had washed our faces afresh, that we set forth with my Uncle Christian to go the round of the Revel. There were a crowd of folks to be sure, but we kept well together, Uncle Christian's broad shoulders making way for us in and out amongst the folks and covered booths where the shows were. All seemed as new and wonderful to our young eyes; again did the donkey fire a loaded gun, and a strange man in green and yellow swallowed fire as though it had been but simple turnip greens, but it was round the cheap-jack's wares that my Uncle Christian made the longest stay, dearly did he love a bargain, and to get the best of the quickest jack in the fair was to him the best business of the show.

Now when we had well been the round, and there was naught left to see but the folks, we felt for the money in our pockets which we had been saving up for many months against the fair, and went off to the booths to spend the same on gingerbreads and comfits. It was while Seth was pondering deeply whether or no he would spend his last penny on sugar-sticks or nuts, that, looking about me I noticed that Vita and Volo were no longer with us.

At length did our Seth make up his mind, and it was with a goodly show of sticky parcels in our hands that we left the booth. And it was while we were making our way through the crowd that the sound of a fiddle playing a lively tune caught hold of our ears, while we saw the folk closing round something in their midst, laughing and clapping their hands the while. Thinking yet there was some wonderful sight to be seen, which Uncle Clemoes had missed, we went along with them till we came along side of a dark foreign looking man who was playing a fiddle right skilfully, while there in the cleared space before him were two folk dancing merrily to the time of the tune.

I could scarce believe my eyes when first I looked, for sure they were no other than our Vita and Volo, and dancing in a manner I could ne'er have dreamed two human creatures could dance.

Volo held a flowering tamerisk branch, a hand on each end of it. Now would he hold it straight out in front of him, and then again high above his head. Vita was opposite him with arms held aloft, while between her fingers in either hand she carried loosely two grey stones from the beach, clacking them sharply together the while to the time of the music. And all the while their graceful bodies swayed to and fro to the measure, their feet going quicker and quicker, as the foreign man hastened the pace of the tune.

Now and again would Volo make a swift bound towards the maid with his tamerisk bush held high; but she with an agile turn of her body in a twinkling was behind him, he turning again as swiftly after her. Ever she seemed bidding him to come, yet bidding go, and still the music played faster and faster, the foreign man shouting "Bravo" and the folk laughing and clapping their hands, while ever their feet kept time to the music, and the maiden's stones to the pace of their feet.

Then it came when the measure was at its swiftest, Volo made a quick bound forward, and in a twinkling his flowering wand was about the maiden's neck, and he held her there captive midst a wreath of pink blossoms, while they gazed at each other laughing and flushed, their eyes sparkling like diamonds.

Lord! how the folks shouted and clapped and called it the fun of the fair.

But Honor Higgs looked black, declaring they were proper mountebanks and a disgrace to Trebetherick.

But they had heard that tune before; somewhere long ago, in that foreign land where they came from, had their little feet kept pace to the throb and beat of its tune. So was their memory touched, the blood in their young veins taking fire at the sound of it. And sure no prettier sight was seen by the folk that day at Padstow Revel.

CHAPTER VI

THE GREY HOUSE ON BRAY HILL

NOW of that which came after, when we of this story grew from children into young men and maidens, I can but tell mostly from hearsay, not having been present at much which befell, or at much which concerned those of whom I am writing. But that which I write is surely truth, for they who have helped me with the linking of things together, were ever truthful of tongue, scorning that which was false. Nor do I think that I have given over vent to my fancies, but have set down as simply as I may that which came to me through growing up amongst the folks, with a just knowledge of their ways, with the same of the sea and the fortunes or trouble which it ever brought along with it.

Concerning Bray Hill I have not yet spoken, but as it hath much to do with those of this story, it be needful that I should say something of it. Sure it is but a bald headland of no great pretensions or height, but rising abruptly as it does out of the sand dunes on the St. Enodoc side of the burrows, it forms a barrier between the lonely church and the sea. The western side of it slopeth steeply down to Granaway Strand, covered with scanty brine soaked turf and thyme mown close as a velvet lawn by countless rabbits which breed there, and honey-combed in parts with their burrows. But to the landward side of its base there floweth merrily a little curling brook, trimmed with blue forget-me-nots, and starred with golden flag blooms in the summer, while in the winter time it be all russet and grey with the wraiths of last year's rushes.

About this stream my mother's cows would feed, for it making a pleasant moisture in the sandy land, the herbage grew the more thick and sweet about its edges.

But to the northwards side of Bray Hill rise the cliffs, not like unto the giant walls of Petire, but yet firm and bold enough to guard the hill against the ceaseless wash of the Bar, which it about faceth. Within these cliffs be many curious caves and hollows, wherein when the tide be high the sea makes ever terrifying thunders and strange mysterious moanings, but when the tide be out, the golden sands stretch smilingly beyond, alive with the whirl and cries of countless sea birds.

Now there is but one hollow on Bray Hill wherewith to break its baldness, and in that hollow, with glassy eyes forever fixed upon the foaming bar, stands a small square house of grey stone. Who built it, or how it came to be there, none can say; but it hath stood there as far back as the memory of the oldest liver can tell you, and it stands there to this day.

That time and tempest have laid but little hold to it, you may tell by the solid way it stands, with never a crack in the hard grey stones, or a rift in the slated roof. There be only one thing which seemingly hath taken a liking to the bare bleakness of it, that strange yellow growth which clings to all the wind-swept houses round about; whether it be born of the sea-brine, or be merely a natural herb, I do not know, but it scarce seems to have the juice of the earth in it, neither doth it savour of green fields or dewy meads.

At the back of the house, against the hill side, stands an ancient group of feathery tamerisk bushes, crooked, gnarled, and twisted into many shapes, but nevertheless able to put forth soft pink blossoms when their time comes. Between the hillside and the house, be a small nettle grown yard, and that be all, while to the front of the house be a level space fenced round about by a low stone wall with a gate of drift wood in the midst. This gate leadeth right out to the head of a stone stairway, cut in the solid rock out of the cliff, the only road to the sea and the sands below. These be "the Steps of Trevennon," and a dark and bloody tale is told of them.

For it was many years afore I was born, that one Michael Trevennon lived in that house by the sea. For often have I heard Honor Higgs and Anthony Guy speak of the same, when seated over the fire at Trebetherick.

That he was an evil man, given to dark and ugly ways, there could be but little doubt, and the folk cared little to have anything to say to him, for there were more vessels wrecked on Padstow Bar in Michael Trevennon's day than could fairly be accounted for. Sure, the folk one and all, would well have liked to have seen him strung up at the four cross roads at St. Minver, but it was left to a higher power to bring justice to Michael Trevennon.

It was after one stormy night, so Anthony Guy did say, indeed just such another as that on which I first heard the call of Tregeagle, that when the day broke a noble ship lay wrecked on Padstow Bar, and when the tide went back leaving it high and dry, and the folks were able to get alongside of her, not a living soul was left aboard to tell how it had happened. The sands were strewn about with wreckage of all sorts, rich and beautiful things of which the folk knew little, lay scattered everywhere. And a short time it took them to gather them up and take them home, for we Cornish folk do hold, that which be sent to the land, be sent with a meaning to bide there. Here and there amid the tangle of ropes, did they come upon a poor body all bruised and mangled, but never a living soul of them all to tell how it had come about.

And it was Anthony Guy himself who searching along the sands came first to Trevennon's steps, and there saw a sight which made his blood run cold, and the sweat to stand out upon his face.

Michael Trevennon's boat was there as usual moored by its ropes to a ring in the rock. But twisted and twined in the rope and locked in each other's arms lay Trevennon and another. Both were dead, and so tightly bound together in the tangle of the rope, and their last grip of death, that those who came to Anthony's call could scarce get them apart. For one hand of Trevennon's was clasped about a watch of gold which hung by a chain to the neck of the stranger, while the other had hold of the haft of a knife which was buried deep in his breast.[23]

This was most surely how they found Michael Trevennon, caught by the coil of his own rope, drowned in the midst of a fearsome deed, at the foot of the slippery stairway, which leads up to the house on the hill.

And it was after this that they who sailed up Padstow river on moonlight nights would hear strange calls from Trevennon's steps, aye, and even did they see the dark of Trevennon's boat rocking in the silver stream of light where the moon fell full. While one whose courage had let him come yet nearer, swore as he had witnessed the sight of Michael Trevennon himself stumbling up the slippery steps yet always sliding backward. He appeared with a heavy burden upon his back, seemingly bent double beneath the weight of it, and ever as he gained a step so did he slip back one, till he fell at length with a bitter cry into the depth of water below.

So it was that all came to shun the grey house on the hill which had sheltered for so many years this man of evil doings, and so it was that it stood there empty and alone with its face and glassy eyes forever fixed on the Bar.

Then came the time when my Uncle Joshua thought fit to

---

[23] Haft: hilt.

purchase it on its being put up for sale. And as it was nigh the Trebetherick land, the cattle feeding in the marsh below, he thought it a likely place for the cowshed, and that the time had gone by for the folks to mind aught of the doings of Michael Trevennon.

But he reckoned wrong as he proved to his cost. For the first man he set there came up to Trebetherick one morning near scared to death, saying he had seen Trevennon as plain as in life, standing at his bed's head with a bloody knife in his hand, and that sleep there another night, naught on earth should make him, for sure the next would see him in his shroud if he did.

And so again did the house on the hill stand empty.

But at last one sunny day in summer, many years after, the doors and windows of the grey house stood open for the breeze of heaven to frolic in and out, laden with scents from the sea, and the sweet thyme on the hill, while the sound of a woman's voice, came softly on its wings, singing at her wash-tub, in the nettlegrown yard at the back.

And sure you may well wonder, after what I have said, who could be found with a courage high enough to take this same place for their home, sure no Padstow man or woman, no nor any this side of Rock, knowing what they did of Michael Trevennon, and how from what the cowherd had said long years ago, he most surely did haunt the place.

And this was so, for the woman who dwelt there was not born on Cornish soil, for she was no other indeed than the strange maid Vita. Vita, the wild waif from the sea, untamed as the sea birds, and fearing naught in heaven or earth, I do believe, saving it was Parson Trehern.

I can see her now as she came out through the open doorway, shading her great dark eyes with her hand, and scanning the sands below, and the thin blue line of the river as it flowed onwards to the sea. Vita grown into a handsome maiden, with the rosiest lips from St. Enodoc's to Padstow, aye and further still, so all the folks declared. Though, I for one and Seth for another, loved more to see the soft rose blush upon our cousin Royal's cheek and the glance of her sweet blue eyes. For handsome as Vita most surely was, the boys were shy to go courting, for folks were beginning to whisper strange things concerning her; whether or no it was just her masterful ways, or the mere matter of her dwelling in the house of Michael Trevennon, or again the evil repute which her brother Volo bore, I cannot say, but 'tis truth the maiden was looked at askance, beautiful though she was.

But the light be growing dim, and how the maid came to dwell in the grey house on the hill, I must needs leave till to-morrow; if so be the Lord spare me another day.

CHAPTER VII
CONCERNING VOLO

I HAVE before told how it was that Vita's brother went with my Uncle Christian Clemoes of Padstow to learn the ship-building. He had by this time been with him there a good four years, though it was a great wonder to all, how my Uncle Christian found patience to keep him there so long. But my uncle was ever a kindly man and ready with help to all lamed dogs which came in his way, and having had great experience with fractious youths through the employ of many a such in his ship-yard, knowing at the same time my mother had anxious thoughts for the youth, he suffered and forgave much which others would have sent him long ago to doors for.

It was that wild temper of Volo's, which we had seen so much of when he was but a lad at Trebetherick, which grew the stronger with his coming manhood, for there was never a fight or brawl on Padstow Quay but what "Devil Volo" as they called him, was sure to be in the thick of it.

And he fought not as we Cornishmen do, fairly with our fisties, for it was ever that knife of his which he would not let alone, and which caused the folk to say ugly things about him. But Parson Trehern who knew more of foreigners and their ways than we simple folk, being learned in their histories and such like, said they thought no more of the knife in Volo's land than we did of the fist in ours. And he told how the wild stoat hath its own way with the rabbit, and night-owl with the mouse. But though all ever turned a serious ear to what Parson Trehern should say, Volo's ways were not such as the Padstow folk could clearly understand, or quietly put up with; for there be a difference you may depend between cold steel and honest fisties. So it was that the folk showed plainly that they had no great liking for Volo and his ways, so that he came to be feared and shunned by most of Padstow Town.

But Parson Trehern he ever preached of patience. Thinking that time maybe would quiet the fiery spirit in the youth, and again, that he being a stranger in the land, it behoved all those who had to do with him to deal the more kindly by him; but as Volo did ever kick out at any wholesome restraint you may be sure it was often a difficult matter for my Uncle Christian Clemoes.

To be sure there was one who had more hold on him than any other human being. But it be ever a dangerous matter for a young maiden to wield such a power, when a wild youth is concerned with it. But so it was that she could check him in one of his wildest passions by a look or a gentle word. For so had it come about that a great love for our sweet Royal had grown up within his heart, which was but little wonder, and but a natural outcome of being near her. For who could bide in the same house with Royal Clemoes, watching her pretty ways about the house or table, or listen to her singing in the orchard, without feeling their young blood stir or heart-beats go the quicker. Not a youth in Padstow I'll be sworn, nor a long ways round it either!

And where Volo loved, he loved with his whole passionate nature, and where he hated, he hated with the same fierce strength. But our Royal did but look on this same love of his with a shrinking fear and dread, knowing full well she could not return it, and fearing the outcome, though she had indeed at the same time for him, I know full well, a kind and womanly pity.

And I came to believe through the after years that this unhappy love of Volo's did more for his undoing than his fierce and passionate hate. So, through the worst of that which came after, have I ever felt some pity for him, knowing in my heart how it mostly came about, and sorrowing that it could have been no wise different.

Now it happened one day when the orchard behind my Uncle Christian's house was rosy with bloom, that pretty Royal was sitting under the moss covered gillyflower-tree, looking like naught else but a fair pink blossom herself. She held a bit of work in her lap, but the needle lay idle. Her blue eyes were looking out afar, while dimpling smiles hovered and played about her rosy mouth.

What her thoughts might be, who can say? Nor would it be fair to be over curious as to the mind of a maid. But from her looks they could not have been aught but pleasant ones, which could so bring that tender look to her eyes, or those dimples about her mouth.

So, she sat while the breeze played in and out of the apple trees, and the blackbird sat singing his song of the spring high on one of the topmost sprays. The blue of the Padstow river gleamed through a break in the sunlit houses below, while the masts of the ships in the harbour showed tall and slender between.

But the maiden was gazing at none of these, she was deep in some sweet dream of her own, which maybe the blackbird's song came through, as it will through dreams, after the long years go and our heads are white with age, bringing us back with the call of its voice to the sweet springtime again, and the love song of our youth, clad in their garments of emerald green, and crowned with snowy thorn.

'Twas so she sat there dreaming 'neath the orchard's checkered shade, while dancing lights played upon the gold of her hair, and the bees sweet humming through the blossoms above, and stirring the white stars of the whitsun flowers which grew in masses about her, sending their sweet scents abroad, and filling the air with the same. And so deep was she in those same thoughts of hers, that she heard no brush through the soft spring grass, as of a step upon the ground, nor did it come to her that anyone was nigh, till a dark shadow fell across the white work which lay upon her knee.

The maid gave out a little startled cry, and looking upwards she saw the tall form of Volo standing above her, meeting the gaze from his dark eyes as she looked through the glinting of the sunshine.

Hastily did she take up her work, and make a pretence to sew. But her hands were shaking and her needle suddenly seemed to grow contrary, and somehow it would not pass in and out just where she had a mind for it to go. Then did a knot come in her thread and she tried to undo it, though it was tied uncommon close. At length, with all her pulling and twitching the thread it snapped in two, and she must needs set about threading another needle. But how could she do so with Volo standing there and watching her every movement. He could most surely see the trembling of her hands, she thought, and that was the very thing she had been doing her best to hide. So after all she had to drop her work, hiding her hands beneath the folds.

Volo had flung himself down on a bed of whitsundays at her feet, and lay there gazing up at her watching her pretty woman's ways. Thinking how fair and sweet a maid she was, and wondering in his passionate young heart, how he could make her love him.

This she knew full well you may depend and maybe it was this same knowledge which had set her hand a trembling. As long as she had her needle to play with she had felt a certain courage in the touch of it, but now she had naught to keep her eyes upon, the time had come she knew when she needs must look at Volo, and hear what he had to say.

They stayed there silent awhile with naught to break the stillness between them but the hum of the bees through the blossoms and the blackbird's song overhead.

"I frightened you Royal," he said, stretching out a hand towards her, "somehow that ever seems to be my way with you."

"Sure you did startle me a bit," she said, plucking a whitsunday and twirling it by the stem, not looking at him the while. "I never knew no person was nigh till you came close against me."

"I bided a long whiles watching you before I came nigh," he said, "but you were pretty deep in your thoughts, Royal Clemoes, never to hear me coming. I'd like to know who your thoughts were about. Not me I'll warrant."

Royal blushed till she looked like the pink rose which clusters about my uncle's porch on the southern side of the house, for she fancied for the moment that Volo had learned her thoughts, the leaning her fair young head against the grey bole of the apple tree, she turned up her chin, and laughed at her own foolishness.

"No, Volo, that's truth," she said, looking him straight in the face at last with a merry glance in her eyes.

"Then who was it?" he asked eagerly, "for I'd like to know."

"Would you now really," she said, with her pretty head on one side as if considering deeply, and the laughter still lurking within her eyes. "Well maybe I think I can tell you, for as near as I can mind, Volo, it should be Grandfer Trefry of the White Horse Inn, and my father Christian Clemoes."

And at this she laughed a merry tinkling peal, such as a brook will give when it runneth over the pebbles, which waking all her dimples up she looked more like a flower than ever.

"Now that's not truth," he answered back, a sullen look coming into his eyes. as he saw she had the laugh at him. "For aged folk set no maid a dreaming with smiles about her mouth."

Royal took up her flower, and twirled it round and round, then set to work to count its petals as if much depended thereon.

"You be learned concerning maids, master Volo," she cried, "and when maybe did it happen that you last saw Dinah Moor?"

Volo muttered something under his breath as he tore up a handful of tender green things by the roots, and flung them from him, then he gave a short laugh, looking up at Royal as he spoke, " 'Twas but last night," he said, "at the Royal George; and folks were dancing and making merry. 'Twas a gay night I can tell you." He looked again sharply at the maid, watching eagerly for some movement of her face, but she was still intent upon the flowers.

"Ah!" she said, slowly at length. "It was but last night: dear me, Volo. Why I could never have believed there were so many leaves in a whitsunday."

Volo reached up from where he lay, snatching the flower from her hand. For he was jealous of all she handled, and her ways were making him wild. Then the maid began to see she was going the wrong way about to keep him away from the one thing which she dreaded. For as she saw the angry flush rise to his cheek, and the frown which she knew well the meaning of show upon his brow, she knew it must needs take all her woman's quickness to get her through with it.

Volo drew nearer to her catching her hands in his, she tried hard to free them, but he held them in so close a grasp she could but let them stay.

"You make me just mazed with your ways," he said, "but I aint the one to let you fool me quietly, that I tell you Royal Clemoes.

Now you'd best say at once, who was in your thoughts awhile gone; for I won't let you go till you do."

Now it was Royal's turn to be angered, as angered indeed as it was in the power of so sweet a maid to be. She caught her hands quickly from Volo's, and clasping them about her knees, she tossed her pretty chin and looked him full in the eyes.

"A maid's thoughts be her own," she cried, with a proud little touch in her tone, "and I keep mine master Volo, I'd have you know." The she shut her rosy lips as though she had turned the key, and moved away from him.

"Royal, Royal, I love you!" he cried, stretching out his arm towards her, with a great longing in his voice and eyes.

But the maid took no heed of his words, keeping her face turned from him, with her hands clasped tightly about he knees.

"Royal," he cried, "do you hear?"

But Royal still sat silent and cold, with her face turned from his.

Volo uttered a passionate cry, and flinging himself down on the flowers and grasses beside her buried his face in his arms.

Royal turned slowly round, looking down on the lad at her side. Her woman's heart was stirred and touched by his pain, all feeling of anger had fled as quickly as it had come; for she knew that the poor lad loved her with the strength of his passionate heart.

But what could she do: what could she do! she thought. How give a love where she had none to give. How indeed could she help in any way at all.

And if any true hearted maid do happen to read these pages, who hath had to refuse a strong man's love, when he deemed that love his life, she will sorrow with our sweet Royal, as knowing much of those things which grieved her maiden heart that sunny day in the orchard.

"Volo," she said bending over him, laying a trembling hand on the dark young head beside her, "don't take on so, for I can't bear it."

He raised himself up and looked at her, his face drawn with pain.

"Love me then," he cried, "love me."

"Ah, but I cannot," she cried, while the tears sprang to her eyes clinging about her lashes, as dewdrops about a flower. "I cannot Volo! you don't know what you be asking."

"Yes, I do," he cried, while his voice was full of the passion within him. "I ask for your love Royal Clemoes, I ask for my life, and, if you give no heed to my asking, I'll go straight to Hell, and you know it."

"Oh, Volo, it be not fair on me to speak like that," she cried in great distress. "You know I have ever given you all the love I could. You know I have tried to check you in your wild ways, and how I have stood between you and my father when he would often times have cast you off. Sure I could not have done more for a brother of my own than I have done for you."

But Volo paid no heed to her words.

"It is you," he went on, "who drives me wild. When you are cold to me then I'd just do anything bad that comes in my way, and when I see you walking home from church with Sam Pengelly, or telling on the doorstep with Seth Rounsevall of Trebetherick, I get wild and mazed enough for anything. And so it be," he said with a bitter laugh, "that the good folk of Padstow speak of me as—the devil—and you know quite well Royal that a word from you would stay all this, and yet you hold back from the giving. Now what be the reason, I ask?"

"Oh Volo," she cried in trembling tones, "I have told you."

"No you have not," he cried fiercely, "but you shall. Now be it Sam Pengelly or Seth Rounsevall of Trebetherick?"

It was as he spoke the last name that the warm red colour sprang to the maiden's cheeks and as quickly left them, left her a white as snow.

She rose from the seat, catching hold of a bough of blossoming apple to steady herself, while he rising at the same time stood there looking down upon her.

"Listen to me," she said, "neither Sam Pengelly or Seth have ever spoken words of love to me." Which was the truth, though she knew the time was not far off when they would most surely speak.

Volo gave a shrug of his shoulders and a bitter laugh. "That be well," he cried, "for mark my words, Royal Clemoes, the day they do speak will be a bad day for one, or both."

Then did Royal make a vow in her heart that happen what might that day should never come about, and turning quickly from him with her head bent low, she moved through the flowers to the wicket gate, which led to the back of the house.

Volo stood there watching, till the last glimpse of her slight form disappeared amongst the green, then strode away crushing the innocent flowers beneath his tread, with an ugly feeling in his heart.

That night there was a wilder scene than ever on Padstow Quay with Volo in the midst of it; for it happened that a foreign vessel lay in the harbour with a rough set of folk on board, and 'twas after a drinking bout at the Royal George that they all got to fighting, Volo using his knife in an ugly way on one of the crew.

But it came that for more reasons than one, they of the ship thought it a wise thing to set sail before the morning dawned, which thing they did, taking the wounded man along with them. So did Volo escape the law, which indeed was not a difficult thing to accomplish in the days of which I write.

But my Uncle Clemoes was greatly angered, nor would he hear

of any excuse in his favour. Royal scarcely trying to thwart him in his resolve that Volo should leave his house and the ship-yard for ever. For she deemed it best that it should be so, for his own sake as well as hers.

So was Volo sent to doors; going from bad to worse, having naught to do, and ever mixing with the roughest folk in Padstow. And Royal watching him pass from her chamber over the Quay, grieved at his altered looks, and the sorrow she knew to be in his heart. Long did she plead with my uncle to help him but once again, and long did my uncle turn a deaf ear to her pleadings. Until at length seeing that the maid was really grieving over it, and through his great love for her, rarely refusing her aught, it came that he gave to Volo the management of a small fishing craft, Volo to have half of that which he should gain. But yet was he firm in forbidding him come to the house, or so much as to set his foot inside its doors.

CHAPTER VIII
CONCERNING VITA

NOW my mother was much troubled and concerned that Volo had now no home whereto he might go, and she also dreaded greatly the thoughts of his coming again to Trebetherick, owing to the wildness of his ways, and the knowledge that when he and Seth came together, there was ever a likelihood of their rubbing the one the other the wrong way about. It happened one day as she and Honor were making butter in the dairy, that she should be speaking of the same, and Vita who was seated in the deep window in the kitchen outside unbeknownst to them both, should overhear that which they spake.

"The Lord alone knows," my mother said, turning the butter as she spoke, "what will become of Volo in the end. But that Christian Clemoes hath shewn uncommon patience by him, doing his duty as a Christian man, that no person can deny. But for a wild youth such as Volo to have no home to go to, is ever an evil thing. Though the Lord knows as I don't want him here to Trebetherick."

"And it b'aint very likely," joined in Honor, giving a mighty slap to the butter as she spoke, "that any other person would want un either, turning everything upsey down with they devil's ways of his. And what the Padstow folk won't put up with, I don't see how Trebetherick should. But I ever did tell as naught but harm could come from picking strange children out of the say. Far better to have let un bide where they was. And bide there they should have if I'd ought to do with it."

"Now there you be wrong Honor Higgs," said my mother. "As the Lord threw them ashore I could but bring them home." And she added softly, "I have still hopes He will send His blessings along with them."

Honor gave a toss to her head and a snort, such as our grey pony will when a fly be up its nostrils, which was Honor's way when doubtful.

"Well, I see no signs as yet," she said, "and I fancy as they blessings be a long time on the road, and if Devil Volo don't mind his ways as they'll bide there altogether."

My mother said naught for a space saving "you're wrong Honor, you're wrong."

But she was used to Honor's ways, knowing she ever said more than she meant; and that outspoken as she was and seemingly rough in her way, she was true to all at Trebetherick, loving them as her own. But I will say that from the first to Vita and Volo she was naught else but contrary and sour.

"Well now, if there was but a cottage about," my mother went on to say, "on this side of the river, and well away from Padstow Town, where he might bide with Vita, while she kept house for him, I'd say but he might go a bit steadier. But there aint such a one to be had, as I can see, saving it be Granny Mably's, and Lord! why she baint dead yet, so what's the good of telling of it."

"No, that her baint," said Honor, "and from all I can see her's likely to bide a long whiles yet, though gone in her eighty-four. But the Mablys were ever long livers."

"Well there be no other," said my mother, "as I can tell by."

"Oh yes there be," said Honor with a laugh. "There be the house of Michael Trevennon."

"Good Lord, Honor Higgs," cried my mother, taking her hands from the butter tub, and staring with scared eyes at Honor; "what ever be you telling! Why there's no human creature in Padstow as would ever put foot inside its evil doors."

But there was one human creature not far away, who had listened with flushed cheeks and quickened breath, to all they had to say. It took but a moment for her to make up her mind, that whether inside Padstow or out of it, that there was one who would cross the threshold of Michael Trevennon's house: aye and cross it too before another sun should rise. And moving softly from her seat, she silently left the place, making her way as fast as her young limbs could carry her, to the grey house on the Hill.

She took the short way over the steep meadows which slope downward from Trebetherick, and across the low lying level past the little church of St. Enodoc, the path taking her onward through the tall sweet grasses growing about the little brook, which floweth so pleasantly at the foot of Bray Hill.

And it came that she passed on her way a herd of my mother's cattle, which were standing up to their hocks in a soft oozy place where the blue forget-me-nots grow, keeping the teasing flies away with the working of their tails.

She paid no heed to them, being deep in her thoughts, but went quickly onward with her face flushed, and a bright look in her eyes. And it was as she was nearing the gate which barreth the bridge that crosses the brook, that she heard a soft lowing behind her, and turning about she saw 'twas the red bull Basan, whom my mother had given her two years agone for saving its life in the marsh.

He came slowly out from the herd, swinging his great front back and fore as he moved, and lowing gently the while. But Vita showed no fear at the sight of him as most maids would have done, but just stood there quiet and still in the path, till the great beast came up with her.

"Ah, my good Basan," she said, "so you could not let your mistress pass without letting her know."

And flinging one shapely arm about him, she laid her cheek against his neck, stroking his shaggy frontlet the while with her hand, while the great beast nosed about her, the same as a dog will when he hath a kindly wish towards you.

"Ah Basan, Basan!" she cried, "you are the only living creature as loves me."

And turning quickly from him she opened the wooden gate, and went swiftly upward over the swelling sand-hills which lead to the Grey House on the Hill.

The great beast stood watching her till she moved out of sight, then turning himself about went slowly back to the herd.

She had found him one day when he as but a yearling near lost in a miry pit in the marsh. For when the rains be heavy the ground below Bray Hill will fill and swell, till it becomes a dangerous place to pass, and at such times the folk take the higher track across the sand-hills. It was at such a time as this that the young bull strayed from the herd, and getting deep into a slushy pit, most surely would have been lost, had not Vita found him and dragged him forth with the help of her strong young arms, and the sense of the danger within him.

Parson Trehern hearing the same took much account of it, saying "Martha, the maid hath saved the life of the beast, and by right it should be hers." So my mother agreeing to the same, Parson did christen him "Basan" after the fearsome bull in the Bible, and Basan he was ever after called by we of Trebetherick. And it came that the beast would follow Vita everywhere, the same as a dog will his master, and the folks much wondered to see it, Honor Higgs amongst the number, not quite liking the look of things. For to others Basan was ever surly and ugly, while to Vita his way was that of a faithful hound to its mistress.

When Vita at length had gained the cliffs above Michael Trevennon's steps, she paused awhile watching the sea below.

For the tide was up and curling waves were breaking against the base of the steps leaving them slippery and slimy to the tread. Stepper Point lay soft in the dim blue haze of the distance, and the sun shone fair on the heaving waters between; while the white gulls wheeled and whirled about, giving out strange cries as they flew.

And away to the right, sure it was a fair sight she looked on. The great headland of Pentire rearing mightily from the flashing fringe of waves, the river's mouth, the sea beyond, and Gulland purple in the haze, standing as a sentinel in the midst; and ever the blue spread of heaving waters between.

"So these be Trevennon's Steps," she said, bringing her eyes back again to the rugged stairway beneath her, "and this be Trevennon's house," and turning quickly about she faced the cold grey front, with the glassy eyes of it staring ever across the restless waters beyond.

She opened the wooden gate in the rough stone wall, crossing the level space between, laying her hand without fear or tremble on the rusty latch of the door.

But it was fast locked, and though she gave more than one strong shake, pushing the while with her knee to help force it, it kept steady and firm, not yielding to her hand. So seeing there was no means of entering by the door, she let it go, and turned about to the window, shading her eyes with her hands to keep the sunlight off, trying to peer in through. But the panes were so caked and frosted with the salt rime from the sea,[24] that her sight

---

[24] Rime: mist.

could not pierce their thickness, and owing to the same she could see naught of what was within.

But Vita was one of those, who when they have made up their mind to a thing, do not give over easily. And she determined that in spite of barred door and windows, get into Michael Trevennon's house that day she would, and that naught should stop her. And looking about for help her eyes happened to light on a grey beach-stone at her feet, and stooping quickly she picked it up, hurling it at a glazed pane in the window.

It went crashing through, sending the splintered glass abroad, and making hollow echoes and sounds through the empty rooms of the house.

The maiden paused a moment, then slipped her hand inside the broken square feeling softly for the bolt, and finding it at length she pulled the stiffened window strongly towards her, and as it moved slowly outwards on its rusty hinges, the breeze of heaven flew in through the open space, filling the lonely house with the breath of the sea, and stirring the dust of years, and the cobwebs which clung thickly to the walls.

Then the maid placing her knee on the sill, flew like a bird in after the breeze. She had got her way at last, and stood there alone with the spiders in Michael Trevennon's house.

Standing there in the midst of the room, she looked sharply about her, now at the dirty corners, and then at the empty hearth, with a few charred logs lying there just as the cowherd had left them. It was but a square bare room like many other, but the wash of the sea sounded through the open window and echoed about its walls.

The maiden laughed aloud and turned herself about.

"So Michael Trevennon," she said, "you h'ant a been here of late, or you'd have made more stir with the cobwebs."

And as in answer the breeze flew in more strongly, stirring the thick brown webs which hung there, and moving them back and forth, till they looked like the ghosts of flitter-bats clinging against the walls.

Vita opened the door and looked into the darkened passage beyond, then crossing it boldly she mounted the stairway which led to the rooms above. There she opened a window and stood for a while watching the sea below, and the ways of the white winged birds.

"Well," she said to herself, "one might do worse than bide in the house of Michael Trevennon." And closing the window she left the place the same way as she had come, speeding swiftly homewards across the marsh, up the steep hillside to Trebetherick.

CHAPTER IX
PARSON TREHERN

WHEN Vita entered the kitchen of Trebetherick, she found my mother sitting in the window in the light of the westering sun, deeply intent on turning the heel of a long blue stocking she was knitting. And the maid, who had come in open-mouthed and ready with what she had to say, stood still in the ruddy glow which came sifting through the flowering fuchsias in the window, flooding the room with its warmth, and at the same time catching hold of the scarlet and orange bandanna about her neck, and touching up the snakey coils of glossy hair turned about her shapely head.

Now they who understand much about women folk will know of this same mystery of "turning the heel," and that at such a time it be ever wise to be silent, nor to make much noise with the pans, or clattering about the room. And I mind that as a youth I had more sharp words from my mother at such a time than at any other, so that I had ever a wholesome dread of this same operation. And as for Honor Higgs! why no person could bide in the room with her when she was so employed.

So Vita having learnt her lesson, bided quiet until she heard my mother heave a sigh, which meant that the worst was over, and making a quiet move forward she leaned herself against the side of the window and began to speak.

"Mother Rousevall," she cried, "I have somewhat I wish to say to you."

My mother gave a start as she spoke, "Lord! Vita," she cried, dropping her knitting to her lap, "what a fright you gave me to be sure! How quiet you must have come in."

"Not so very," said Vita fingering at a fuchsia-bell as she spoke.

My mother took up her knitting again, and began to count the stitches. "You be more like a cat than a maid," she said.

"There's no need for every person to tread as hard as Honor Higgs," said Vita, giving a toss to her head and snapping off a fuchsia-bell as she spoke. "But Mother Rounsevall, I have somewhat to say to you, which will not wait in the saying."

My mother laid down her knitting again, looking up to the flushed and eager face above her.

"And what be this mighty bit of news," she said, "as cannot bide till I have finished the turning of my heel."

"This," said Vita bending fore, with her breath coming quick. "Will you let me go and live with Volo in Michael Trevennon's house?"

"Good Lord!" cried my mother with a gasp, "you're mazed!" And she sat there staring at Vita as though she saw the mermaid of Padstow herself. Then she said slowly, "Now whatever could have put such a thought into your mind?"

"None but you and Honor Higgs, but a few hours agone," the maiden answered hotly. "For I heard every word you were telling in the dairy Mother Rounsevall; and I gathered pretty fairly from the same, that Trebetherick would as soon have my room as my company, and would give no place to my brother Volo willing or unwilling. Where Volo goes, I go! and 'tis many thanks I give Honor Higgs for naming the house of Trevennon."

My mother's face had slowly flushed, as Vita spoke of overhearing that which passed between her and Honor that day, but at the name of Trevennon her cheeks turned white as the muslin cap about her face.

"Never speak of it," she cried, "never speak of it. None that

I have aught to do with shall dwell in that evil place. What be you telling of Vita? Why no human being since the herd has ever crossed its doorstep."

Vita threw back her head and laughed, while my mother stared at her open mouthed.

"Oh yes there be," she said.

"Who?" cried my mother.

"Why I myself," she said, giving a toss to her head, "and but this very day. Oh but I have," she said with a nod, answering the look of doubt on my mother's face. "I could not get in by the door, so I did by the window. I went all over the house, yes into every room, but saw naught of Michael Trevennon, and naught of his ghost. 'Tis just the very place for Volo and me."

And again she laughed, as she followed up the words my mother had spoken.

"Do you mean to say as 'tis solemn truth, Vita, as you've entered Michael Trevennon's house this day?"

"Aye, 'tis truth, every word of it," the maiden answered quickly. "Not only did I enter it, but went into every corner, and room. And moreover looked down on Trevennon's steps, and chose in my mind the place where Volo should moor his boat to, the very place I reckon where Michael moored his."

"Lord, Vita!" my mother cried, "don't talk like that there! you're too free with your daring ways, and sure some evil will befall you, before you come to your end."

"Mother Rounsevall," said Vita, bending nearer, "let us have that house. You will get rid of those you do not want, and they will be content."

"Never," cried my mother with passion. "Never! for evil will only come to they who bide in that wicked place. The Lord forbid that I should ever have any hand in sending a human creature there."

Vita rose from her seat. "Be these your last words?" she said.

"Yes, they be," said my mother slowly.

The maid raised her arms, and clasped her hands above her shapely head, and looked down on my mother.

"Then I go to Parson Trehern," she said. "And turning on her heel, moved in her silent way quickly across the room, and out at the open door."

After she had gone my mother sat there awhile thinking of many things. For indeed she was greatly troubled that Vita had overheard what she had said that day, and the way the maid had taken it, also at her desire to leave Trebetherick behind. But through all of it comforted her much to think she had ever done her duty by her.

Yes truly, she had ever done her duty. But there was one thing she had never done, my mother, that was to give her love to those strange children brought to her by the sea. Duty be one thing, but love be another, and to my thinking there be a great difference between the two. To be waited on and served by a sense of duty, is not the same as to be waited on and served by love. I have known it and felt it. Therefore do I feel for Vita in her proud desire to leave Trebetherick behind.

For there were but two human beings whom my mother had ever given her love to. The fine young husband whom the sea had washed up years agone on Polseth Strand, and my handsome brother Seth, who so much favoured him. But to the rest it was naught but duty, which is a fine thing, but be but cold and chilly when compared with the warmth which love doth ever bring with it.

Meanwhile, the maid Vita was speeding along the steep pathway which winds upwards through the furzy combe to where the village of St. Minver stands high upon the hill-top.[25] The sun was dropping behind her as a blood red ball into the shining sea, throwing a rosy blush over headland and sky and land, the little twisting stream below showing here and there 'neath the shadows of the furze brake, as a crimson ribbon will when twined amid the dark tresses of a maid. The soft murmur of the sea came upwards from the strand and the song of a thrush from a privet brake across the combe.

But the maid took no note of the fair beauty of the setting sun, nor of the voice of the singing bird, but went swiftly onwards with full thoughts, nor did she stop once to take a breath till she came to the white gate leading into the parson's garden.

It was there that she found him, busily watering a bed of tall white lilies, intermixed with "bloody warriors."[26] He had taken his coat off for the purpose, and had bound his red bandanna about his brow thinking thereby to protect it from the small evil gnats, which do mar the pleasantest garden, and are ever more vengeful as the sun goes down.

The parson loved his garden dearly. He spoke of the flowers as his children, and sure he took as much thought and care for them as they had been human creatures, even going so far as to reason with them at times, as if they had the sense to understand.

"Ah Vita," he said, as she came up, "you know where to find me."

"Well I reckon Parson," she answered, "you'd be tending your flowers as usual."

"Aye," he said, "that's right. Tending my flowers as usual. For they are but children you see, my maid, and wanting a father's care,

---

[25] Furzy: furze-covered. Furze, gorse.

[26] Bloody warriors: deep red wallflowers (*Erysimum cheiri*).

or they fall into trouble. Now look at that lily there, she opened her flowers so fast that she made herself top-heavy, the thoughtless thing, and had I not been handy with a good straight hazel rod and a bit of string she would have broke her back mayhap; and all the beauty she has taken so much care and thought to bring about would have been laid low in the mire. Ah well, " he said, as he flicked out the last few drops of water from his can, "these children of mine, they are but as other folks' children after all."

The soft breeze blew in from the sea, setting the "bloody warriors" moving gently to and fro and stirring up the many sweet scents from the garden. The night moths hummed and fluttered about the flowers, while the music of the singing birds sounded clear and sweet from the orchard nigh at hand.

The parson had filled his can again from the well close against the sun-dial, and again he was busy emptying it, the soft patter of the falling water sounding pleasantly on the leaves of the thirsty flowers.

"Now look to those pansy flowers, Vita," he went on, "their little faces ever turned upwards to the sky, some laughing, some crying, not one of them with the same look, saving it be their colour. They are good children these, giving little trouble, though they suffer much at times, indeed they suffer much from that evil beast the slug. Oh! I have to be watchful I can tell you, in this same sweet nursery of mine. There now, I will put on my coat for the dews be falling and they have a way of finding out the weak places in a man, and we will to the summer house, where I can rest my old back, and take a taste of my pipe."

And Vita who knew full well that it was no more use her trying to have her say with him while still intent upon his flowers, any more than it was with my mother when deep in the matter of her heel, followed him to the honeysuckle bower neath the twisted quicken-bean, and bided patiently while he slowly lighted his pipe, and with much comfort was puffing the first few full whiffs of it forth into the scented air.[27]

"Parson," she said, laying her hand on his arm. "I have something to say."

And she told him in quick eager tones, of her visit to the house of Michael Trevennon that day, and then of her request to my mother, and her refusal of the same.

"Parson," she said, "I cannot bide at Trebetherick any longer. There is no love for me there. There is no love for Volo. We are not wanted."

Parson Trehern made no answer for the moment, but sat quietly looking out beyond him to where the tall lilies stood as slim white ghosts in the gathering dusk, while the night beetles boomed amongst their petals swinging away through the dimness of the apple orchard beyond.

"Once," he said, "I tried to grow a southern cactus amid my homely pansies: but it withered and died. I reckon it sighed for the hot sun of the south, nor could it stand our cold Atlantic breezes."

"Ah," cried Vita, "that is indeed so with me. I cannot live! I cannot live without that which I cannot have."

Then again a silence fell upon them and there was no sound without but of the soft winged creatures of the night, and the rustle of a dreaming bird in the quicken-bean overhead.

"Maid," said the parson, "I will tell you a story."

"Once there were two lads living under the same roof. One of them was as handsome as the day, and bubbling over with fresh

---

[27] Quicken-bean: Rowan tree.

young life as our Polseth brook, and the other was but a crooked stick and somewhat queer maybe in his ways. And the handsome lad had all the love that was to be given from the first, while the crooked one had naught, though God knows he craved for it badly enough, and gave it richly where he might. And it came that these two lads should grow to manhood, and that they both did give their heart's great love to the same fair maid. The handsome youth he won her, and the crooked one hid his face and went forth amongst the shadows. And amongst these shadows he met with many a sad soul, who like himself had hidden their faces and gone forth from the garden of Eden, having the greatest gift of God denied them. They were ever wandering along a darkened road, seeking for that which they might never have. Then a great pity arose in the heart of the young man for these same wanderers, so that he dwelt amongst them, striving with all humility to bring what small comfort he might to those poor travellers along that strange mysterious road, which the Lord in his wisdom had thought fit to lead them."

The parson's pipe had gone out unheeded. He sat with his hands on his knees looking far away beyond the misty flowers, far, far beyond the summer dusk, into the long, long years agone.

The tears stood in the dark eyes of the maid. Parson had touched a string in that proud young heart which had ne'er been stirred before.

Ah, she thought, he knows! He understands. She laid her warm young hand on the wrinkled one on his knee.

"Help me Parson," she said.

The parson roused himself, and gave a look to his pipe.

"I will speak to Martha to-morrow," he said, "you know where to come, my maid."

"Aye," she said as she rose, "I know where to come." And leaving him she passed through the sleeping flowers into the soft stillness of the summer night with a gentle comfort at her heart.

CHAPTER X
THE HARVEST HOME

IT was harvest time at Trebetherick. For many a week the ripening grain had spread all golden and smiling to the edges of the sun-scorched down, showing fair and rich against the blue dazzle of the sea.

It was that year, owing to the extreme heat, and the rain having fallen kindly at the right time, that the corn harvest both at Trebetherick and elsewhere fell extraordinarily thick and heavy.

Now after the last load had been carried in, it had ever been our custom at Trebetherick, to give a fine supper to all those good friends and neighbours of ours, who had helped the ingathering. There would be the Pentire Head folk, and those of the Glaze, with many others from Polseth, with their women folk attached; not forgetting our own kin, and the kindly presence of Parson Trehern, without which last no Harvest Home at Trebetherick would rightly have been blessed.

Sure there was one other who was ever bidden, he being Peter Pengelly of Padstow, it being his business after the supper was cleared away, and the old folks made comfortable with their pipes, to set the young folks a-dancing with the help of that wondrous fiddle of his. And indeed I think that these homely gatherings would have been but dull affairs without the presence of Peter Pengelly of Padstow.

For I ever noticed, as he laid his head with kindly affection against the body of his little fiddle, and with the help of his bow, drew forth the first long note or so from its strings, as a warning to all to get themselves in readiness for the first jig; that tongues which had hitherto been silent or tardy in their work, began to wag, and shy eyes to sparkle and dance, as if the music had already set them going.

And to me it has ever been a strange and curious thing, the magic which lies in cat-gut.

And that night all did fair justice to the supper my mother and Honor Higgs had prepared, not that I can ever mind their doing otherwise, for Cornish men are brave fellows with their knife and fork, and a life on the Cornish cliffs will go further to make a man hearty, than any doctor's medicine.

And it was after Parson Trehern had given thanks to the Lord for all His mercies, and especially for the bounteous harvest vouchsafed to Trebetherick that year; that my mother with the help of the maidens was not long in getting the supper out of the way; and the youths in lifting back the oaken table and chairs so as not to incommode the dancers.

The old men grouped themselves about the doorway, and set to with their pipes, enjoying meanwhile the pleasant cool of the evening after the toil and heat of the day. For it was but the early part of September, and the air warm and soft, as often comes with that same time of the year, with the gentle breath from the sea blowing softly across my mother's garden, filling the air with the sweet scents of the myrtle blossoms which bloomed there is great abundance.

Now of all the sweet maidens brought together that night by the Harvest Home of Trebetherick, sure none was so sweet or fair as our gentle Royal Clemoes. Clad all in white, with no bit of colour about her save the golden brown of her hair, and the rose bloom on her cheeks. Ah! but I remember the dark green leaves of the myrtle midst the kerchief on her breast, while it shed about her the scent of its blossoms like the flower that she seemed.

There were two pair of youthful eyes both full of love and passion, which followed her every movement whithersoever she went, the blue eyes of my handsome brother Seth, and the dark ones of wild Volo.

And maybe that she felt them upon her, though to outward appearance she seemed to have no knowledge of the fact. But surely there be no maid in creation who can have the flame of love so near and yet be unconscious of its warmth.

And so she moved about in her lightsome grace, helping my mother with her sweet woman's ways. Volo was ever close at her elbow when a heavy dish must be lifted, or a empty jug to be filled. And Seth feeling his own slowness grew angry at himself, and still more with Volo, while a wrathful frown gathered on his brow, making me fear that trouble would come between those two hot-headed boys before the night was out.

Like some strange foreign bird, clothed in blue and yellow, Vita in her quick way flitted here and there, watching those three with restless eyes, from beneath the dark shadow of her brows.

And now the room was clear, leaving a fine space in the middle for the dancers. And it was time for Peter Pengelly to tune up, while the old folk in the doorway sat telling of their dancing days.

'Twas how Farmer Coats of Pentire had challenged one of Polseth in bygone years to step-dance. And how he of Polseth had given in full five minutes by the clock, before he, Farmer Coats of pentire, had so much as thought of flinging out his last kick; his wind being as fresh when he had to give over as when he had first set forth, and he of Polseth being reckoned the best step-dancer this side of Padstow too.

"Ah! dancing baint the same now as it were in my time," he said with a solemn shake of the head. "The young folk baint such fine men as their forebears you may depend."

And though he seemed to take it thus sadly, yet it appeared to me that it comforted him much at the same time to feel that it should be so.

"Sure I reckon it be but early in the day for the Straats of Lunnon," Farmer Coates went on, "the cannels would look a bit waake yet awhile I fancy; but us must have it afore the night's out.[28] 'Twouldn't be a proper Harvest Home without the Straats of Lunnon."

"Never fear, never fear! Farmer," said Honor Higgs who was passing by at the time. "I've a fine lot of dips ready as I bought at Padstow myself, and I've cleaned up the brazen cannel-sticks so as you'd see your way to shave in 'em.[29] You'm a bit too hasty Farmer a-asking for the Straats of Lunnon afore the dimsey falls, that you be."[30]

Then Peter Pengelly laid that fiddle of his most kindly against his cheek, and drawing his bow across it brought forth a few sweet, wondrous notes, which set the maids' hearts beating and brought the colour to their cheeks.

Ah, Peter Pengelly! Peter Pengelly of Padstow! you and your fiddle have indeed much to answer for. Playing havoc with maidens' hearts as if you were tossing meadow grass, and taking no heed of the consequences.

A pleasant sight it was to be sure, to see those brave Cornish lads and maidens lining the old brown walls of Trebetherick while

---

28 Straats of Lunnon: Streets of London. Cannels: candles. Waake: weak.

29 Dips: dip-candles. Brazen cannel-sticks: Brass candlesticks.

30 Dimsey: twilight, also dark.

they made themselves ready for the kerchief dance, catching at the gay bandannas which joined the man to the maid. Sure! many an old heart thrilled at the sight, remembering the days of its youth, while Peter Pengelly set them agoing with the magic of his fiddle.

I can see them all now as if it were but yesterday, the bending and twisting of the youthful forms as they twined in and out amidst the gay network of bandannas. The glancing of bright eyes, the loosing of bright locks as hand met hand in the gladsome movement of the dance.

"Ah, 'tis well to be young," said Parson Trehern with a sigh, " 'tis well indeed to be young."

From dance to dance they went with scarce a pause between, for Peter Pengelly's finger bones seemed made of wroughten steel, and the young folk having no thought of tire, though 'twas after a long day's harvesting, mid the heat and glow of the fields.

Ah! 'tis well indeed to be young.

So the soft dim light of evening spread over all, till it came to be time for mother and Honor Higgs to set about getting the lights ready.

"Wait a bit, and don't ee be in too much of a hurry mistress," said Farmer Coats. "Let's have the Straats of Lunnon first, I say. 'Tis dimsey enough now I'll warrant to see the city folk fine with all their pretty caperings."

"You're right Farmer," said mother, " 'tis dimsey enough to be sure. Honor you'd best be getting the candles ready against the Straats of Lunnon."

Now I have heard it said, though I cannot repeat it as truth, that this same dance of the Streets of London be but little indulged in outside our county of Cornwall, though other folk have told me that they have frequently taken part in the pleasant pastime in the neighbouring county of Devon. But if this story should travel beyond, (which I feel it scarce likely to do) maybe it would be a kindly thought to those who would know something of its curious ways, to relate the manner in which it was danced that same night in Trebetherick kitchen.

It be somewhat a lengthy proceeding that same lighting up of the streets, for each man and maiden must have their separate candle, and tallow be ever a slow thing to inflame. But it was accomplished at last, and Honor with just pride, placed her shining candlesticks, all with their lighted candles, in two comely rows upon the floor, leaving space enough between them for the men and maids to stand. Then Peter Pengelly started them, and away they went.

In and out and out and in between the lights, the men and maidens capered, meeting at the end with clasped hands and coming down the street to the tune of Peter's fiddle. And never a maiden touched with her skirts the flaring light or the dropping grease, but catching at her frills as she went in the way a woman will, showing her feet as she tripped, with just enough of her shoe and stocking.

"Well done, well done!" shouted Farmer Coats, as he stamped on the floor the time of the jig, with the help of his nailed boots. "Mistress, mind your petticoats when the grease begins to run."

But no need had Farmer Coats to give the maids warning, for surely if a frill or a skirt had so much as touched the candles their fair name in the Streets of London would for ever have been lost, and the maid who burnt her petticoat would never more find a partner.

So on and on tripped the dancers, and on and on fiddled Peter Pengelly, till the lights of the—Streets of London—flickered and flared in their sockets, with many a splutter and hiss, then one by one went out, leaving the young folks breathless and laughing, while the smitch of burning tallow dimmed the air.[31]

Sure it was after this same dance that the young folk felt a longing to enjoy the cool of the night, and by ones and twos strolled forth into my mother's garden, and amongst them hand in hand just as they left the dance, went my bother Seth and our dainty Royal Clemoes, these two last finding their way amidst the fuchsias and myrtles into the jasmine bower beneath the beeches.

Now it was strange that Royal Clemoes should so let Seth take her by the hand, and lead her away from the rest into the shadow of the bower. For a long time now she had shunned and avoided him, not giving him so much as the chance of a word or a look, leaving him restless and discontented, so that my mother looked anxiously on him.

But there she was now seated close beside him, seemingly forgetful of all her proud ways, and content that he should so hold her hand, and gaze into her eyes with all the love and desire which a man can only show for the one sweet maid he loves.

Ah! Peter Pengelly of Padstow, you have indeed much to account for.

Why even then he was busy weaving spells with that little fiddle of his, for out through the window came the sound of its sweet complainings, softened by the distance, and borne outwards through the myrtles till it reached the dim shadow of the bower.

It was at Peter Pengelly's call that the young folk came trooping backwards and in at the open door, once more to join the dancers, leaving the garden silent save for the wail of the distant music,

31 Smitch: smoke.

the faint murmur of the sea, or the cry of some late sea bird as it winged homeward through the night.

"Royal, dear, lift up your face and look at me. I want to see your eyes."

And Royal with Peter Pengelly's witchery still upon her, lifted her head and looked, and so looking let him twine his strong arms about her, till her fair head rested on his warm young heart.

So they sat there in the silence, happy in the mere nearness of each other, in a dream almost too dear for words. For love surely needs no fine speeches to tell its meaning, a touch of the hand, a glance from the eyes, and all is known, yes, all is known.

"Ah my darling, my sweet," Seth murmured low, pressing his lips to hers in one long kiss, "I love you, how I love you."

But Royal lay still in his arms, and spoke no word, while the murmur of the sea came upward from the shore.

"Sweetheart," he went on, "how long I have loved you! from boy to man, and yet have been afeard to tell you so before to-night. Maybe you have thought me a mighty fool for my bashfulness. Eh now, and have you? And of late I have been so jealous and near mad with that poor devil Volo, thinking you were slighting me for him. But it was not so, my sweet, it was not so, was it?"

He bent his eyes to hers as if to find the answer in her face. The beech trees over head trembled strangely in the still air, as if they too would hear the answer. But Royal lay there still and silent on his breast, and answered him never a word.

A sudden fear took hold of him. Why did she lie there so still and quiet, with her face as white as snow, and her sweet eyes near closed, and not a word of love from her lips, not one little word.

"Oh Royal! my little sweetheart," he cried, "what is the matter? You are not frightened dear? No, not frightened of me, not of Seth!

Oh speak to me darling, speak to me. Tell me that you love me. Tell me that you love me maiden, only that dear one, just that you love me!"

And again the beech trees seemed to shiver as if trembling for the answer.

Royal raised her head from his breast, then slowly loosed her hands from the pleading hold of his, firmly pushed the loving arm from about her, that again and again would enfold her.

"You must leave me alone," she said in a strange low voice, "No you must not touch me. You must not touch me again."

She rose and tottered to the side of the bower, as one just recovering from a mortal sickness, no trace of colour on her fair cheeks, and a look of awful fear in her eyes, seeming scarce able to stand with the terror that was on her. She twined her hand about with a loop of twisted jasmine, and seemingly, but for the hold of it, she must have fallen where she was. A shaft of moonlight streamed through the entrance, and fell on her where she stood, white as a churchyard ghost, with that look of fear in her eyes.

"Seth, you must go away from me, go away at once."

Her words came hurried and hoarse, as though a strangling hand were held about her throat. Seth sprang from his seat and looked down at her.

"Go away from you!" he cried, his voice trembling with pain and passion. "No I will not go away, Royal Clemoes. Why should I go? You love me, I know it. You have told me so this night though you spake no word in the telling. No," he cried again, setting his lips together, "I will not go, I will not!"

"I do not love you Seth Rounsevall."

"My God! you lie."

A dead stick from the beech tree over head snapped off

short and came rattling down on the woven roof of the arbour.

He gripped both her arms with his strong young hands, and gazed long upon her face. There was a stillness in the arbour so as you might have heard their hearts beat, while the maiden's slender form quivered beneath the strength of his hold. But again she said in that strange low tone.

"Seth Rounsevall, I do not love you."

"Royal my darling, say you do not mean it. Oh sweetheart, dear, say that you do not mean it."

And such a world of anguish rang in the words he spoke, that Royal shook beneath them as a flower 'neath the wind.

But again she spoke in a voice so low he scarce could hear the words, "Seth Rounsevall, once for all, I say I cannot love you. Go, for heaven's sake go."

"My God!" he cried, almost flinging her from him. "You of all women, Royal Clemoes, to treat a man like this. You false and cruel maid. That I should ever say it. Go! I will go, and mark my words, you shall see my face no more."

And so he flung away and left her, his great chest heaving with the pain and misery within him. Away into the stillness of the night, away from his sweet Royal Clemoes whom he held so dear, away from old Trebetherick, nevermore to return.

And Royal stood there alone, with her hand pressed tight against her heart, as one in mortal pain. Then God had mercy on her, letting her lose all knowledge, so she fell white as her own myrtle blossoms, blessedly forgetful for a time of the great sorrow which had come upon her.

The sound of Seth's footsteps had scarce died away, or the clang of the wooden gate falling to had scarce broken the stillness of the night, when the crouching form of a woman rose silently from its hiding-place behind the arbour, and making her way to the entrance, stood for a moment gazing down on the maiden within. Then bending low, took the sweet pale head upon her knees, gently wiping the cold moisture from her brow, and touching the silk of her curls.

"Poor little maid," she whispered softly, "poor little maid."

And the beech trees shivered no more that night for the evil spirit had left them.

"Ah well for you Seth Rounsevall!" he laughed. "Well indeed for you to go."

The woman raised her head and held her breath to listen.

Steps moved towards the garden gate, the way Seth had taken, paused there, then turning went inward toward the house.

"Thank God," murmured the woman. "Brave maiden." And then she knew!

CHAPTER XI

THE VISIT TO ST. MINVER

AND it was for many a day after that same Harvest Home, that our Royal lay as one without speech, on the white bed in my mother's best room at Trebetherick. And to all who came and questioned her she seemed as one who was deaf, lying there still and silent, as white as the linen sheets beneath her, with that look of fear in her eyes.

And none would she have about her but the strange maiden Vita, whom before she had shunned and shrunk from as though she had almost feared her. Not even my Uncle Clemoes whom she loved so dear, nor Honor Higgs, and least of all my mother. For if the last did but enter the room she would cling to Vita with little cries and moans, until my mother seeing how her presence grieved her, let her have her way, though she could in nowise understand it.

Now all that we heard of that night's doings at Trebetherick was from Vita, and that was little indeed. How she had found Royal prostrate on the ground of the jasmine bower, and had heard the quick click of the garden gate and the sound of a man's steps stumbling downwards on the stony road to St. Enodoc. This was all, and scanty news we thought it. But it came from Padstow later, that a boat had put in that night from a foreign vessel outside in quest of hands, they being short of the same. But finding none ready to go, had waited till the tide came in and the moon was us before starting. And as they were about to push off, one of Padstow who was on the quay at the time, had seen a man jump on board, and the foreign men went off with him seemingly without question or word.

When my mother heard this news, she stood for a time most strangely still, and her face turned ashen grey. Then raising her head she cried aloud "He hath had the call as his father had before him. Oh Seth my lad! my lad! Oh Seth my boy!"

It was so that my mother took the going away of Seth. The sea had "called" for her boy, as it had for her own heart's love, for so it had ever been with us of Trebetherick.

So she took up this new sorrow along with the old one, carrying it about with her day's work, but speaking little of it, though age seemed sudden to have laid its heavy hand upon her, showing this second burden was greater than she could bear.

The days and weeks went by, and still Royal lay there on her bed, in that same silent way, with the look of fear in her eyes, having no other about her but the maiden Vita, who was sorely troubled and distressed how to rouse or help her out of this same curious sickness.

And it came to her one day suddenly, as she was leaning with her elbows on the window-ledge, gazing down below at the sun lit downs and the shining sea beyond, as it leaped and played about the purple crags of old Pentire, that then and there she would rouse the maiden from this strange lethargy into which she had fallen.

"Dear," she said rising as she spoke, "let me put you in Mother Rounsevall's chair by the window, where you can see the waves run in on Granaway Strand."

And not waiting for the answer, she took the maiden in her strong young arms, and folding a warm wrap around her, placed her in my mother's chair beside the window.

"There," she said, "now it will do you good to look out a bit."

They sat silent for a time. Royal looking outwards with dull eyes, seeing, yet not seeing the blue of the sea with the pleasant sunlight upon it, and the white sail out beyond. Vita sat busy with her knitting, yet now and again casting a quick glance at Royal from beneath the dark shadow of her brows.

"Mother Rounsevall thinks that Seth hath had *the call*," she said at length. "And all in Padstow and Polseth do think the same, and that is why he hath left Trebetherick behind."

Royal started, the colour rushing to her white cheeks as Vita spoke, her breath came quick, and catching hold of both arms of her chair she leaned forward to the maid.

"That is not why Seth Rounsevall hath left Trebetherick," she cried, her face one quiver as she spoke.

"You see," went on Vita as though she had not heard the maid's words, "it seems but natural, for so many of them have had the call. There was Seth's father, he did the same, leaving wife and child behind, and why should not Seth too have heard "the call" that same night in the murmuring of the sea."

Ah the murmuring of the sea! The murmuring of the sea! Would Royal ever forget it, as it came sifting through the jasmine bower that night, mingling with the sound of Peter's fiddle and the sweet scents of the myrtles. Ah, the murmur of the sea, would it ever, ever cease."

She put her hands to her ears as if to shut out the sound of it, then leaning forward looked out of the window. Away on the bright blue sea was a little silver sail. And her thoughts flew off to Seth, sailing away from her, far away from all, away from old Trebetherick, and all he held so dear. A tender light came to her eyes, and the tears welled slowly up till the sea grew blurred and dim, and Royal dropped her head upon her hands, and wept as maidens will when their heart's love hath gone from them.

Maybe he had heard "the call," maybe it was not all her doing, which had sent him forth that night. And yet in her inmost heart she knew this thought would never comfort her. For most surely it was her doing.

Then Vita seeing her tears and the softened look in her eyes, rose quietly and left her alone.

From that day our Royal began to gain her strength. Day after day would she sit at her window watching the blue of the sea, and the waves dance on the shore. While Vita at times would take her forth along the Polseth Road, but never into the garden or near the jasmine bower. And she grew patient with my mother, who would speak to her of "the call," and how Seth had but done as his forebears, and none could gainsay him. But though she would so listen to her words, the look of fear would come to her eyes, and Vita seeing it, would clench her two hands tight, moving away from the room, as she could not bear the sight.

It was near the middle of October, one of those bright, clear days with a frost in the early morning, when Vita and Royal did plan they would go to St. Minver, if so be Royal's weak state would allow her to travel so far. For Abram Isaac had long a chair of Vita's mending, which she would never get back unless she went to see after it. They crossed above Polseth and up the same pathway Vita took that day when she went to visit Parson Trehern. The grass was wet with the morning's rime, and the heath and bramble brakes all spangled with gossamer webs.[32] The heath-flowers were mostly brown and dead, but here and there a patch of purple still showed and the gorse was yet in blossom. The robins sang in the privet brakes that day, for the thrushes' song was over, but the Polseth brook babbled and laughed below them

[32] Heath: heather.

the same as ever, dancing out between the yellowing ferns, and the mellowing reeds and grasses.

The maidens went but slowly on their way, for the path be rough and steep up the combe to St. Minver, and Royal through her weakness must needs stop now and again to gather fresh strength to go forwards. They spoke but little, their thoughts being full. For the sight of the sea as it came in on Polseth Strand, and even the way they were taking, filling their minds with thoughts of one who had so often trod it with them. And so it was they spoke but little, but as they lingered reached the late hazel nuts which the boys' sharp eyes had left behind, or gathered the few last blackberries which frost and birds had spared.

It was so at length they reached St. Minver, and the white gate of the parsonage over which Parson Trehern was leaning, enjoying his pipe and the pleasant air from the sea.

"Now this is a good thing indeed," he said, "that Royal Clemoes should be about again, and able to climb up the hill to St. Minver. Come in my dears. Come in and sit you down, and I'll find a glass of mead for you, made from my own honey, and I'll promise you will find it sweet."

"Oh thank you kindly Parson," said Vita, "but we must not be staying, for I have to see Abram Isaac about a chair of mine as he has had this long whiles, and we must be getting back."

"No, no," said Parson, "I will not hear of it, for Royal Clemoes looks faint and weary; and rest she shall, though Abram Isaac did keep your chair for ever, maid."

"Well," said Vita laughing, "maybe 'tis best for Royal to sit a bit, I can go on to Master Abram, Parson, and call for Royal on my ways back."

"So do, so do," said Parson as he opened the gate. "Now

little maid, you come with me and rest awhile till Vita has done her business!"

And Royal who was indeed looking sadly after her long climb, followed him slowly along the garden path between the Michaelmas daisies, and through the panelled passage into the parson's parlour.

And there he sat her down in his own chair beside the fire, loosing her bonnet strings with his own hands and putting it aside for her as tenderly as a woman. Then he himself fetched glasses and a bottle, and poured out the mead of which he was so proud.

"Oh Parson, you be too kind," said Royal, "to take so much trouble for me."

"Tut tut," said the parson, "and who shall I take trouble for I'd like to know if it wasn't for you. I don't get the chance every day I can tell you to have a pretty maiden sitting in my chair, or the chance to untie her bonnet strings."

"You'd soon be tired of it if you had, Parson," she said with a little laugh.

"Well maybe I should, my dear, maybe I should," he answered as he carefully wiped the cobwebs from the mead bottle with the help of his bandanna, "maybe I should, but I cannot say for I have never yet had the chance to try it. Now you just sip that mead, Royal, and see if it don't bring the roses to your cheeks."

Royal did as she was bid and nearly choked at the first sip.

"It is rather strong, isn't it Parson!" she said.

"Not a bit of it my dear, not a bit of it. Now just you take another, and it will make a different maid of you."

He leaned forward with his hands upon his knees, anxiously watching her over his spectacles as she took it.

"Now what do you think of it?" he said.

"Beautiful," she answered, daintily tasting it with her lips.

"Ah," he said, "it makes all the difference how you feed the bees, there's no better honey in all St. Minver than mine, that I'll declare, and so no better mead. But you must keep it, Royal my dear. That's the secret, why that mead you're tasting is six years old if it's a day. That's the secret, my dear, you may depend."

But at that moment, when he was well on this hobby of his, Thurza his old housekeeper did call him from the room. And Royal left alone, her thoughts flew back to the dear days when she and Seth did come to St. Minver to taste the parson's mead together. She clasped her hands tight and a weary look creeped over her face, nor did she hear the parson return, she was so far away in her thoughts.

He came to her and gently smoothed the hair from her brow.

"My dear, you must not look like that," he said.

"Oh Parson I can't help it," she cried, and hid her face in her hands.

"My child, you are too young," he said, "to take your sorrow like this. It is your first, dear maid, and you must not let it break your heart."

"Oh Parson," she cried, "but I love him so."

"Poor little maid," he said, "poor little maid." And there was a great tenderness in his tone.

"Oh Parson," she cried, laying her hand on his and looking up to his face as he bent beside her.

"Sometimes I think I must tell all, tell, or I shall go mad. But I have to keep it all to myself, for how else can it be!"

"I cannot tell Vita, though she has been so good, I cannot tell any one, because, oh I dare not!"

She hid her face again in her hands, trembling in every limb.

"And why not tell Parson Trehern," he said, "surely he is old enough to keep a secret, Royal."

"Oh!" she cried, looking up at him quickly. "If I could, if only I could."

He laid his old hand tenderly upon Royal's young one. "Tell me all about it my dear, and don't be afraid, it won't seem so dreadful after you have once spoken, that I'll warrant."

"Oh, but it is dreadful, Parson," she cried, "you don't know, you can't tell how dreadful it is."

"Now you try," he said coaxingly, "just you try, and tell me all about it."

Royal pressed her hand to her heart, and took a quick breath.

"Oh," she cried. "It began that day in the orchard, when Volo told me of his love. But I knew it long before that when I come to think of it, for Volo was ever jealous of Seth."

"Parson," she said looking up at him, "you mind the time that Volo come to bide with us, and you mind he was ever wild in his ways and how he troubled my father. But to me he was gentle, and, and I alone could check him in one of his ways, or in some wild thing he must do."

"And I was always so sorry for him, oh so sorry; and it did not come to me until too late, that it would have been kinder to have been hard where I had been gentle, and thoughtless where I had used thought. But how was I to know, Parson dear."

"Yes," she said, "it came to me most surely that day in the orchard when Volo told of his love. It was only last spring, Parson, when the apple-trees were in bloom. And oh! I was so sorry for him. But what could I do but tell him that it could not be, for I knew in my heart that I loved Seth Rounsevall, and could never love another."

"Then he said bitter things to me Parson. 'It is that devil Seth Rounsevall that comes between us.' "

"And I answered him that Seth had spoken no words of love to me, which was the truth."

" 'Mark my words,' he said, 'the day he does 'twill be the worse for him.' And I saw murder in his eyes as he spoke, yes Parson, murder."

Royal paused a moment to moisten her parched lips, and then went on again.

"And I made a solemn vow in my heart, that Seth should never speak those words, for I knew it would mean death to him if he did, and now," she cried, spreading out both her hands, "I have broken my vow, I have broken it."

"But oh I bided a long time first Parson, it seemed a long time to me. For all this summer I was cold to Seth, even letting him think it was Volo I liked, so that I might save him. But it was cruel hard. I had always watched for him as he passed along the street, looking upwards for me, in my window over the porch. But after that day in the orchard I was never there to greet him, but hid behind the curtain, seeing naught but anger and disappointment on his face as he passed along."

"Then after all this striving, came that night at Trebetherick, when I undid all, I forgot all. What came over me I cannot tell, but there was no one there that night for me but Seth, and I in my foolishness let him see it."

"It was after the—Streets of London—that he took me by the hand and led me to the jasmine bower, and I let him so lead me without a word."

She pressed her hand to her heart as though to still its beating, and her breath came quickly from between her lips.

"Oh I was so happy," she cried, "when he took me in his arms, and told me that he loved me, and I was content to just lie there and listen to his words. And it was so resting in his loving hold that I looked upwards to where a shaft of moonlight fell through the open lattice-work above, and then I turned to stone where I lay; for gazing down upon me where the moon shone full upon it was an evil, evil thing, with a gleaming knife in its hand. The form and face of Devil Volo with murder in his eyes."

"I could not move," she said, "I dare not speak, and all the while Seth was telling his words of love to me, while those awful eyes were looking into mine."

Her voice sank so low, that the parson could scarce catch her words, and the look of fear was back again on her face.

"I closed my eyes to shut them out," she said. "I felt I must think, think. But my mind it would not move, that evil sight on the beech tree above had turned it to stone, I was near dead with fear."

"Still Seth spoke of love, while I knew that every word was heard by Volo overhead, and that every word he spake might be his last, and yet I could not stir."

"And though I had closed my eyes, I still could see that wicked form above me, with the gleaming thing in his hand. He will kill him! He will kill him, I thought: and maybe it was that which helped me to put Seth from me, and to use the only words which might keep that evil from him."

"I do not love you, Seth Rounsevall, I said, and never, never can."

"God forgive me! I lied, but what else could I do."

"And Seth! oh, I scarce mind what he said, words of love and words of bitterness. But I said naught but I do not love you, feeling each time I spoke them I stayed murder for a moment."

"And Seth at last flung away from me in anger. Seth, my love! But I spoke no word but let him go. And I shall see my dear no more."

Then the tears came at last, as the parson knew they must. For the telling of that night's work, must needs strain the maiden sorely. And these same tears of womenfolk are strange mysterious things, which though they come through sorrow, bring comfort in the shedding. This the parson knew full well, so let her be, soothing her hair the while with his kindly hand, till her sobbing grew more gentle, and she lay quiet in her chair.

"Drink this, my dear," he said, reaching for the glass of mead, which the maiden had just put aside all but untasted. "Drink this and dry your eyes, for Vita will soon be returning to take you home to Trebetherick."

The maiden raised her tear stained face as he spoke, and did as he bid, wiping her eyes the while with a trembling hand, with the kerchief which he gave her.

"Brave little maiden," he said. "Brave little maid. It was through your woman's wit, my dear, and that good lie which was such trouble to you, that you saved Seth Rounsevall's life that night, and another from mortal sin. Have courage, my child, your Seth will come back to you again, never fear. The sea may call for the Rounsevalls, but it brings them back again, it brings them back."

And he thought of one flung up on Polseth Strand at a loving woman's feet.

"But Volo," the maiden cried with a frightened look in her eyes. "Oh Parson, he will be here."

"Who knows! who knows," said Parson Trehern. "He may be here to-day and gone to-morrow. He is but a restless spirit Volo, I doubt if he stay long in this quiet corner of ours."

Yet he thought in his mind, where Royal is Volo will be, and he feared in his heart for the maid.

But he had quieted Royal greatly with his words of comfort.

"Oh Parson," she cried with a restful sigh, "sure I do feel better for telling you."

"That's right my dear," he answered kindly. "I thought maybe you would. Ah, here comes Vita. It is getting late in the day, and you must be going back before the evening gets too chill."

Vita came into the room, glancing quickly from one to the other. "Abram Isaac keeped me telling," she said, "so I am a bit late. Royal, we must be going at once, my dear, or Mother Rounsevall will be getting in a way at my keeping you out so late."

Royal rose putting on her bonnet, feeling lighter at her heart than she had for many a day, and together with the parson they went out to the garden gate.

"Vita," said Parson Trehern, as he bid her good-bye, "I put Royal Clemoes into your care."

Vita met his eyes with a steady look. "She is in my care already, Parson," she said, and taking the maid's arm in hers, turned from him and went homewards down the hill.

He leaned on the gate, and stood there watching them until the bushes hid them from his view. "Yet another shadow," he murmured, "the road is strangely thronged," and he turned slowly to the house, with his eyes bent upon the ground.

CHAPTER XII
STRANGE DOINGS

THE dark drear days of November came along, and with them hurried mists and sweeping rains, driven inwards by the western wind, wrapping the headlands in their watery hold and mantle of grey, shutting out from the Padstow folk all sight of what lay beyond.

Time dragged heavily for Royal, as day after day she sat in her chamber over the porch, listening to the ceaseless patter of the rain, while painful thoughts came to her the more fully for the shutting in of the mist.

Now and again, when the pattering on the pane near made her mad, she would fling the casement wide to let the full swift drift of the rain drive against her, what matter if it soaked her face and hair, it was better than that ceaseless patter with the closed window, which shut her out from everything. So would she lean sometimes when the early twilight fell, and the lights on the quay or harbour showed out one by one, blurred and dimmed by the heavy mist that hung around. So would she scan the faces of the sailor-men, as they loafed or swaggered along the quay, searching for that one face, dearer than all else on earth to her.

At times a visit from Vita would go far to break the slow dullness of the day; but it was but rarely that the maid could so venture, owing to the care that she must take that Volo was off and away before she dare set out. For of late he had been strange in his ways, hanging about the land, nor going off for a day or two in his boat as he used, and oft-times questioning her sharp as to her doings or where she had been, and as to her comings and goings.

So it came that her visits to Royal were far and few between, but it cheered our Royal greatly when the door burst open and Vita's bright young form, clad in her long blue cloak, with the scent of the sea about her, stepped lightly into her room.

"Ah, my dear! 'tis a blessed sight to see you," Royal would say. "You brave maid to come. I've been near mazed to-day, Vita, with my thoughts and the driving rain."

Then she would take the maiden's cloak and hood to the kitchen fire to dry. So would they sit together hand in hand, talking as maidens will, till the dusk began to fall, and the time came for Vita to make her way homeward, across the ferry and onwards over the misty burrows to the house upon the hill.

Vita had warned Royal to travel no distance from home. Well the maid knew the reason, that it was in the fear that Volo would way-lay her. Rarely in those days did she venture far from her doors, save on some homely errand or to see the ships come in. Once or twice had she come across him in the town, but had turned her head aside with the pretence that she had not seen him, not before she had caught the angry scowl on his face, and a look which made her tremble. So she clung the more closely to her chamber over the porch, waiting and watching with little hope in her heart, through those dark November days.

And the maiden Vita from her window in the grey house, also watched and waited, and her heart went outwards on the same errand as our sweet Royal's. But at the same time her mind was troubled and clouded, with a mystery nearer home, which with all her quickness she found a difficult matter to unravel.

For Volo had been strange in his ways of late, and these same ways puzzled and troubled her much, so that she could not make out how to take them. For as I mentioned before he rarely went a' fishing now, and as far as she could tell he was ever away on the cliffs, starting away in the early morn and not returning home until the darkness fell; and then he would have no word as to where he had been or what his business might be. For many an hour would he sit silent over the fire, then again would he let his wild spirits go till he seemed as one possessed.

So she watched him quietly as day after day he disappeared into the mist, the while asking no question, though fearing much and puzzling sore, as to what this strange business of his might be. For to sea he did not go she knew from the smell of the earth which was ever about his clothes, and the snared rabbit which now and again would fill the pot for supper, and besides this his boat was ever moored to the steps below, proving he had no use for the same.

But the maid was not one of those who bide still long and let things take their way. Had she not given her word to Parson Trehern to keep watch and ward over Royal Clemoes. Evil was in the air, that she felt; for these secret ways of Volo boded no good to himself or others she knew.

So it was that she set her woman's wits to work to discover this same mystery, and day after day when Volo had left her without a word, and she had watched his form grow dimmer and dimmer as he took his way downwards to the hollow beneath the hill, that as the grey drift closed on him she hastened with breathless speed to the summit of the mound above, stumbling amid the dripping tamerisk bushes and burrows till she came to the ruined chapel of St. Nectern, whose loose grey stones still crown the hill. There she would crouch to gain her breath waiting for the mists to lift so she might scan the valley below, with the track across Granaway Strand and the downs which lay beyond. But never once had the drift arisen to give her a fair look-out.

So would she sit amid the dripping stones and rotten fern, while all around her, beneath her and above, hung the blank grey curtain of the mist, shutting out all but the dripping pile where she crouched, and the rough edges of the stones against which she leaned. She could taste the salt brine which the wind brought to her lips. She could hear the moaning of the sea below, and the cry of wandering sea birds winging blindly through the waste, but the curtain of the heavy mist ne'er lifted once to show that she sought for.

But at last the dull drear days of November came to an end, and crystal frosts began to crisp the grasses in the swamp below, and to stiffen the dead lean teazle stalks and ragwort on the hill, though near to the sea the frost be ever slight. But nevertheless slight as it was, it banished the mist from land and sea, bringing along with it brighter days with a freer outlook to those who watched and waited.

Now it happened one afternoon nigh unto Christmas-tide, when twilight was just coming on, that Vita was gathering in the clothes which she had set out that morning to dry on the tamerisk behind the house, when the sound of the bull Basan bellowing and carrying on in the mead below came to her ears. What might be the meaning of it she could not tell, but most surely was he greatly disturbed over some cause or another. So hastily gathering in her clothes she ran quickly down over the sand-hills to see what this same disturbance might mean.

'Twas as she neared the grey stone wall that she caught sight of something which stayed her in her course, and crouching low she creeped under the kindly shelter of the tamerisk bushes to the shadow of the wall, and keeping well behind it, watched with keen eyes that which was passing on the other side.

It was on the opposite side of the little brook, where the firm ground reaches to the edge of the swamp that the bull Basan stood. By the glare of his small eye, the lashing of his tail, and by the mighty bellowings which he now and again sent forth, he was showing in every way that anger had got the best of him.

Below him standing on a tummock of rushes, with his back turned to the place where the maiden crouched in hiding, stood Volo. From one hand a rope was dangling while the other he held out in a coaxing fashion towards the angry beast. That he had been driven thus far by the creature, Basan fearing to go yet farther after him owing to the memory of what had befallen him, through that same swamp in his youth, was most clear and plain to the maid. But the strange thing seemed to her, that Volo also knowing the same, did not at once cross the swamp and so put himself altogether out of the furious creature's reach. Instead of which he continued to coax and call, holding forth the corn he held the while, and speaking in gentle tones to the beast.

But it was all of no avail, indeed it seemed but to infuriate Basan the more. For suddenly the bull flung his head upwards with a vicious jerk, then lowering his horns made an ugly rush down the bank to where Volo stood in the swamp.

The moment the beast's forelegs struck the swamp, he fell forward with a heavy thud, burying his nose in the mire, then raising his head and struggling mightily the while he bellowed forth again and again with mingled rage and fear, then with a heave of his heavy body he struggled to his feet, finding himself once more with the steady ground beneath him.

As Vita watched the bull make that downward rush of his towards the swamp, her heart-beats grew quicker, for she feared for Volo. But it was as the beast lowered his head that Volo took a step backwards, and in a moment was also deep in the mire, struggling and swearing lustily the while at Basan and his ways. Vita then seeing that no further harm could come of it than a muddy coat, and maybe a spell of bad temper, creeped from her hiding place, and wended her way homewards as quickly as she might.

And long did she think and wonder about that she had witnessed, for what could Volo be up to with that rope and handful of corn, trying to get round Basan when he knew that the beats could never abide him. But that he had some purpose in his mind she felt but little doubt, and the thought came over her that she must needs be more watchful and wakeful than before, for most surely there was some strange mystery abroad which she alone might unravel.

CHAPTER XIII

ANTHONY GUY AND THE SHIP OF SPAIN

IT was Christmas Day at Trebetherick, and I mind that same afternoon, Parson Trehern had preached to us in the little Church of St. Enodoc, one of his moving deliveries, using the Word for his text "Peace upon earth, good-will towards men." Sure I had meditated much on those blessed sayings, while on the road homewards, seeing that towards such and such a person whom I could name, that this same good-will was a mighty difficult matter to give. But nevertheless my heart seemed the larger for his holy talk, and I felt a great desire to see no harm in any man or woman, even to excuse Volo's strange ways, on my way that Christmas Day across the sand-hills.

Now we had no gay doings that Christmas-tide at Trebetherick which had ever heretofore been our custom. For Seth being away, who indeed was there to make merry for? So the time coming round of this same season which brings all together, seemed but the more lonesome for his absence. So that my mother had said, "We will have no gathering this year, we shall but miss the lad the more."—And she put her apron to her eyes and went out into the dairy where I knew she was having her cry out.

But this could not prevent Honor from making the Christmas Pudding, or hanging up a branch of holly over the clock, or putting on that wonderful cap of hers with the purple ribbons. Nor indeed could it prevent her and Anthony Guy, after the supper was cleared, drawing their chairs to the blaze, and telling at length of things which had come to pass in the years gone by.

Now I had out my paper and pen that night, for it was my habit at the end of each day, to set down when the house was in quietness all that happened and the thoughts that came to me through these same happenings. Those of the household were used to my ways, and took no heed of my sitting there, seemingly wrapped up in my pen and my thoughts. I had dipped my pen in the ink, and was thinking out a well turned phrase wherewith to commence a clean page, my mind running strongly on the sermon of good Parson Trehern, when my ears caught that which straightway sent it out of my head, and dropping my pen softly on the table, I rested my head in my hands as though deep in thought, but in truth I was listening to that which was going on beyond.

"No person knawed where Michael Trevennon he put it tu, and no person knaws to this day." And Anthony Guy thumped the wooden arm of his chair as he spoke, and began slowly to fill his pipe.

Honor was sitting squarely on her chair, her hands clasped tightly on her lap, with her strange and wonderful Sunday cap upon her head in honour of the day, the purple bows with which it was decked standing stiffly out on either side of her head, strangely like unto the holly trimming on the clock, which stood in the corner behind her, indeed I think she must have had that cap in mind when she placed the bunches there.

"No," said Anthony again, after with much difficulty and many grunts he had set his pipe going with the help of a lighted straw. "No, no person knows to this day."

"Lord, he must have put it somewheres," said Honor, "that's certain sure."

"Aye, that's certain sure," said Anthony slowly clearing his throat, and spitting into the fire. "Certain sure Honor Higgs as he put un somehweres, but where's the thing as I should like to find out."

"My, now wherever do 'ee think it could a' bin," said Honor.

Well she knew the answer, for she had heard it a hundred times before, but it is the way with our west-country folk as it be with children, they do dearly love to hear the same story over again, and though they may know by heart every word of that which is to come, still they listen afresh each time, as though they had ne'er heard it before.

And Anthony Guy looking mighty wise, and as he were telling the story for the first time, took his pipe from his mouth, and leaned forward to Honor where she sat, dropping his voice as he spoke, as he feared some person might overhear him.

"Well, I'll tell 'ee what the folks did say, as he'd got it all buried out there, under the kitchen floor to Bray Hill."

"Get along with 'ee," said Honor with wide eyes and uplifted hands.

"Iss they du," said Athony solemnly nodding his head as he spoke. "Iss they du."

The soft rain sapped and sucked against the window, while the wind sobbed gently round the house, for it was a rainy Christmas-tide such as often comes to us in the West, and Anthony pulled again at his pipe, and they sat for a time in silence. For Anthony ever took much time in setting off, though once well on the road it became a difficult matter to stay him.

"But," said Anthony Guy at length, "I don't believe a darned word of it."

"Don't 'ee really," said Honor.

"Not a darned word," said Anthony with great force, "don't tell me as he could iver git it all in, dig and bury as he might, Honor Higgs. I tell 'ee he could never git it all in."

"Lord," said Honor. "Now what be yu telling of."

"He was a darned sight too many years at it," said Anthony slowly, leaning forward and marking off his words with his pipe stem, "a darned sight too many years at it, Honor Higgs, you may dipend."

"Tu be sure," said Honor, "he weren't so wonderful young when yu..... But Lord a mussy, us had best not be telling about it," and she looked back over her shoulder, and drew a bit closer to the fire."

Again the wind cried about the house, and the rain sucked and sapped against the window, and they sat silent for a space. Honor staring with wild eyes at the fire, and Anthony pulling at his pipe.

"You may depend," said Anthony again, "that dig and bury as he might, that there Michael could niver have got it in. There was that there Spanish ship, Honor Higgs, as would have filled that there kitchen-floor up to Grey House, as much as three times over. There was things aboard that ship, Honor Higgs, as you've niver seed in your life, tables and chairs just a rinning all over with solid gold, an' jewgs an basins, with cups and saucers of the same, which would make your eyes open pretty wide, Honor Higgs, I reckon, if they ever did catch a sight of the same."

"Jewgs and basins, tay cups and sarcers of gold," cried Honor with a gasp. "Lord, who ever heard tell of such things. Now Anthony Guy for sure you be telling up lies."

Anthony Guy took his pipe from his mouth, and thumped the arm of his chair.

"If 'twas the last word as iver I spake," he said, " 'tis gospel truth, for I see'd them with my own eyes. Aye," he added, "and there was more than that, aye, a pretty sight more nor that."

"Now whatever could there be," cried Honor breathlessly.

"Chains of gold a shining like the sun in all his glory," cried

Anthony Guy, now fairly on his road, "bales of silks and satins, all colours, an lace as fine as gossamer webs, as ud make 'ee stare Honor Higgs if you'd a once set eyes on un, I can tell 'ee, and other things as I couldn't put no name to, niver having see'd aught like un before, and not knowing the same."

"Good Lord," cried Honor sitting back on her chair, "sure 'tis past all believing."

But believe every word of it she most surely did, and that I could see.

"Now there was only me; only me and one other," Anthony Guy went on, "as see'd and knowd aught of they things. Only me and one other, and that there one being Michael Trevennon himself."

"There was two ships as came ashore that night, 'twas a heavy fog as you couldn't see your hand afore your face. The first ship her comed in t'other side of Stepper Point, and drawed most of the folks away from our side. And this here Spanish ship no person saw aught of till her'd abin many hours high and dry on Granaway rocks, leastways no person but Michael Trevennon and me."

"I'd a had to be up early that morning, I mind, after a young heifer as had strayed away the night afore in the mist, and Farmer Joshua was afeard as he might a valled over cleve.[33] I was out on Granaway Down, when 'twas yet dimsey, and come sudden on the ship jambed high and dry in a cleft between two gurt rocks, just as the say had a left her."[34]

"I stude there for a bit an looked at her, but it weren't a long spell neither I can tell 'ee, Honor Higgs, afore I'd climbed aboard to see what her was made of."

---

33 Valled over cleve: fallen over a cliff (or the steep side of a hill).

34 Gurt: great.

Honor felt that now the time had come in this story of Anthony Guy's, when an interruption on her part would be strangely out of place, so she merely sat open-mouthed staring at Anthony Guy, to show she missed naught of the wonderful thing he was telling.

"There weren't no sign of any living thing on board," Anthony Guy went on, "nor I tell 'ee of any dead ones, as far as I could see, and I reckoned as they'd tuked tu their boats afore they'd rounded Pentire, and so maybe had come to their end, or gone to some other place."

"And after I'd luked about above, I thought as I'd see what sort of place it might be below, though I didn't half like the thoughts of it, I can tell 'ee, not knowing what I might come against. That strange craft with the stillness of things, and the queer luke which they grey light gave to all about it, made one feel a bit strange I can tell 'ee, Honor Higgs."

"Now as I was a groping and feeling along a passage, for it got darker as I went down, I stumbled and varled over summat as lay in the road, and stooping down I feeled for what it might be, an most sure for the moment I feeled mighty queer, for 'twas the body of a man I had varled across, and his dead hand which I'd a tooked hold of, though still warm to the touch."

"I stepped across him, and feeled about with my hand and got hold of a handle to a door, which I turned, an it opened quiet like letting in a stream of light on that poor dead thing at my feet."

"He was as handsome a man as ever yu see'd, dressed properly fine, with rings on his hands as shone and shone again. That he'd only just gone home and had met with a bloody death, I could see plain, for the blood was oozing slowly from a nasty gash in his throat. I all but turned and ran for I didn't like the looks of it. But a noise in the cabin beyond made me turn about and look. My! what a sight to be sure! It near tuke my breath away, I can tell 'ee."

"There, standing agin a table, just a covered all over with jewgs and dishes of living gold, a lighted up with a light as hung from the cabin roof, with his back turned to where I stood, was Michael Trevennon. In his hand he held that which sent out a light as the very sun in heaven. I tell 'ee as I could scarce bear the dazzle of it in my eyes as I luked. 'Twas a long sparkling thing a flashing out bits of light in a way as I'd niver seed afore. The whole cabin round was just one blaze of scarlet and gold, but the most powerful thing I seed, and I could not take my eyes from it, was that there shining sparkling thing as Michael Trevennon held in his hand, and that there hand was gashed about in an ugly way, the red blood dripping from it to the goldy things below. Then I knawed as the man at my feet had made a fight for it, and as Micheal Trevennon as he always did had a gotten the best of it."

"An Michael Trevennon he was so taken up with the thing he held, that he never so much as heard me lift the latch of the door, nor guessed but what he was the only one aboard that precious ship. And I, thanking the Lord that it should be so, stepped back quiet over the body at my feet, and crep softly along the passage and out of that hellish place, and mighty thankful I was I can tell 'ee to see the sky and to feel Granaway limpiters a scrunching under my boots, for sure I valued my skin a bit too highly in those days for I tu interfere with Michael and his ways."[35]

"Lord! 'twas a mercy indeed," said Honor, "as he never turned and saw 'ee."

" 'Twould have been the last day as I'd a seed," said Anthony

35 Limpiters: limpets, small marine snails with cone-like shells.

slowly refilling his pipe, "the very last day as I'd a seed, Honor Higgs, yu may depend. For Michael he'd always got his knife along with him, and I'd naught that day but my two fisties."

"But did the volks see nothin 'tall of it?" said Honor.

"Nothin 'tall," said Anthony, "nothin 'tall I tell 'ee, for when they got aboard 'twas some hours arter, and there weren't no signs of Michael Trevennon, or no dead body as I ever heard about, nor never a sign of they goldy things, as I seed so plain, nor of that same shining thing as I seed a dangling from his bloody hand. Never a sign."

"But however he got it all tooked off in time has been ever a marvel to me, nor what he did with it, or where he put it tu. For the volks guessed who'd abin afore un (though bless 'ee I'd said naught about it). But where he carred all his stuff tu; no person knows to this day."

Honor turned on her chair and looked at Anthony Guy. She half opened her mouth to speak and then seemed to think better of it, and they sat awhile in silence, while I waited for more to come.

"What be devil Volo doing out over tu Pentire Head," she said at length, "day after day in the mist, and night after night in the dimsey, always out over tu Pentire Head?"

"Lord knows," said Anthony Guy sharply, "I doant."

"Maybe," Honor went on, "as Michael he might have had hiding places out that ways about, who knows as what devil Volo mightn' have come across something as had set un on the track."

"Thee be a vule, Honor Higgs. A great vule, to tell of sich a thing," Anthony said. "Why I knaws every nick and cranny out over Petire Head, aye up the coast for a mile or more; there baint no sense in that anyways."

Honor nodded her head, and looked as though her mind

was that Anthony Guy did not know everything.

"You men volks always thinks as yu know all," she said, with a snort through her nose, "but that there Volo's after something wid his trampings back and fore, I'll be bound."

" 'Taint Michael Trevennon's goods then, I'll answer for it," said Anthony. "Volks aint sich vules here-about but what they'd a found them afore this if they'd bin Pentire ways about."

At this Honor had naught to say, and they sat silent again, while the wind sobbed around the house, and the rain drove against the window pane.

But this talk of theirs had set me thinking. Thinking if Honor's woman's wit may be had hit the right nail upon the head in spite of Anthony's words that her thought had got no sense in it. It set me thinking that here indeed might be the answer to Volo's strange journeyings in the mist, and I sat late that night over the dying fire, pondering on what they had said.

CHAPTER XIV
ON PENTIRE HEAD

IT has ever been a pleasant thing to wander by myself about our coast, loving the sounds of nature and the thoughts which only come to a man when alone under God's sky with the sea spread out before him.

Most often my ways took me along the sandy burrows, for dearly do I love their golden swells crowned by silver rushes. Many and many a day have I passed amongst them, lying in a sheltered hollow, content to gaze at the wondrous ribbings of the sand, the work of the playful breeze, or to watch the fleecy cloudlets sail onwards over the blue of the sky, as the white sails do across the sea. Hearkening to the murmur of the waves beyond, and the blessed singing of skylarks overhead.

At times would I take the other way about, up over the track behind our house which leadeth to the little hamlet of Polseth, wandering on the yellow sands awhile, or across the downs of Petire Glaze, to the great head itself. But the sand-hills had ever the kindliest attraction for me, with the glimpses of the winding river flowing onwards to the sea.

But since that same Christmas night, of which I have afore told, I seemed drawn ever in the other direction, and day after day found me wandering Pentire-ways. I did in no ways account for it to myself at the time, but since it has come to me, that doubtless those words of Honor Higgs, had sunk much deeper in my mind than I noticed.

It was on a pleasant day in April, such a one as often comes to us in the West Country, that I was resting awhile on the grey granite crag which crowns the summit at the outmost point of the great headland of Pentire. Above the sky was blue, flecked over with little white clouds a chasing each other in a merry way with the help of the breeze which came after them. Below me the heaving blue of the waters with the purple islets of Newland and Gulland in their midst, fringed around with a white edging of foam, and beyond again the great level of the sea, spreading away and away, shining and flashing under the bright April sun.

Looking over the dizzy edge of the crag, I could see the churning waters, leaping and licking, hundreds of feet below, and the whirlings of nesting gulls.

Away to the west of me the laughing waters 'neath the purple headland of Trevose, and nearer yet came Stepper, with the river's mouth and the golden show of the sands; to the east of me our Cornish coast seemed as though it could have no end, stretching away as it doth for forty miles or more, till it ends in Harty Point, lying like a hazy cloud upon the sea. I could see every crick and cranny of the jagged rugged crags of Boscastle, Bude and Morwestow, and fair they looked indeed in the clear light of that April day.

But fair they be not always, as who should know better than I who from a babe remembered Honor crooning over the fire, when the wind began to blow.

"From Padstow Point to Harty Height

Be a watery grave by day or night."

"Lord! Lord! there'll be many a poor soul as ul go to the bottom twix thick and that this night I reckon. Sure I wonder who'll feed the children."

And my mother would make answer.

"Ne'er saw I the righteous forsaken, or their seed begging their bread."

At which Honor would toss her head and murmur under her breath; "that he couldn't seed so wonderful far, and for sure whoever said it, had never come Padstow ways about." Then my mother would chide her gravely for doubting the Scriptures; while I in my youthful mind wondered much who righteous might be, and if sailor-men were always such.

Now after I had taken my fill that day of all which lay below and beyond, I arose and found my way between the granite crags and over the short green turf toward the eastern horn of Pentire, and here I rested awhile again, and did meditate long on the wondrous scene before me. For at this place the cliffs drop sheer for many hundred feet. And the sea below is deep and of a marvellous green, and here from the scarred side of the cliff below one great spire of granite rears its mighty height against the blue, crowned and patched by that orange growth which you may see along our coast wherever the salt rime drives.

And from a boy I had a great love for that same spire of granite which stood so bravely above the fearsome depths below, forever by itself in the wind, the rain, and the storm, and through it many thoughts came to me that day, as I rested under the shelter of my rock, with scent of April in the air.

I must have bided some time with my thoughts turned inward, when I was suddenly aroused to my usual outlook by a sound which came upwards to me from below, though it seemed to me somewhat to the right. It was not the call of any sea bird, nor that of a wind-hover after a rabbit; naught indeed but the angry swearings of a much befuddled human creature.[36]

I crouched low under my rock making no movement, wondering

[36] Wind-hover: kestrel.

much in my mind what the same sounds might mean, for few folks ever go Pentire ways, saving it to be a shepherd now and again after the sheep, and rarely indeed have I crossed their ways in my wanders.

Again the angry sound came to me, as if 'neath the edge of the cliff to my right. I held my breath and watched, but I had not long to wait. Above the green level of the turf came the hand of a man, which gripped the tough grass tightly, then another hand which clawed into the earth. I was so close that I could see the veins standing out as thick as cord, showing the strain which was set upon them. With the help of these hands a man at length raised himself breast high to the brow of the cliff, and flinging himself face downwards, wriggled as a long-cripple will through the grass, till the whole of him was on safe ground.

And quick as he was, I knew the man beneath me, no other indeed than he I had been unknowingly hunting down for the last three months past.

The kindly dusk was beginning to fall, I crouched lower in my hiding place and waited for what was to come.

He lay for a moment or so, and I could see by the heave of his body that he was panting heavily. After a time he gained his breath, and turning over raised himself up, wiping the moisture from his face, and muttering beneath his breath the while, but I could not catch his sayings. And I crouched the lower in my hiding place scarce daring to breathe.

A little breeze came up from the sea, and brought the sounds my way.

"I was darned near it that time, anyways," he muttered.

Near to what, I thought.

He rose to his feet and looked about him, and took a few steps towards the place where I crouched.

"There's another way in from the top," he muttered, "another way in I'll be sworn. He couldn't have heaved it in from below, though he might have heaved un out. But darned if I hant a had enough of it this day."

He paused a minute as if undecided which way to take, then turning sharp to the right went off around a granite bouldered mound, and was soon lost to my sight.

I watched for awhile thinking maybe he might return, but he seemed to have had enough of his seeking, for I caught no sight of him again as I crept from my hiding place, and went slowly homewards through the dark with many thoughts in my head.

Now it was the day after that I waited on Parson Trehern at the Parsonage House at St. Minver. For I felt myself too feeble a creature to combat alone that thing which had come to me out on the Pentire cliffs, and I knew that his wise head and safe advice would help me much with that which was best to be done. And surely it was while we were seated together in the arbour, that I spoke to him all which and happened the day before out over on Pentire Head. He listened the while offering no remark, saving a kind of grunt now and again, as if to mark more clearly in his mind that which I was saying. And when I had plainly finished, he took his red bandanna out and proceeded with much care to rub up his spectacles, much in the same manner as he did that day of the Delabole slate, which way of his, I discovered in after years, did greatly help his thoughts when a difficult matter was set before him.

"Ill gotten gains," he said at length. "Ill gotten gains bring no blessing in their wake. What good were they to the evil man who stored them? What good are they now? Buried as they be in the bowels of the earth, and tempting another human creature with the lust for gold. Aye the lust for gold."

He rubbed again at his glasses, peered at their shining surface as though he would find there that for which he was searching.

"No," he went on, "I do not think that the lad will find it." And his eyes looked as though he had forgotten my presence, and he gazed out over the garden as though looking into the past.

"No," he went on slowly, "I do not think he will find it, for was it not most carefully hidden, most carefully indeed."

And a thought came over me as I sat there in the arbour, that there was but one person who knew the way to Michael Trevennon's cave and that person no other indeed than Parson Trehern of St. Minver.

"The lust for gold," he murmured again. "What will it not bring a human creature to do! Most surely that boy would go mad at the sight of it. For I know the nature. Let the earth keep it. Most surely if he could get his heart's desire he would spend it all on her. But he cannot get her. He must never have her. She must wait for Seth. Strange, strange are the ways of the Lord, and stranger those of man, but stranger yet be the ways of the devil; may the Lord save us from the same."

He sat with his hands loosely folded on his knees, his bandanna hanging from between his fingers and fluttering in the breeze, his glasses fell to the ground unheeded, and I stooped to pick them up.

Then his eyes came back from the distance and looked into mine. "Ah, thankee lad," he said. "David boy, I am getting a stupid old man, and I fear that my mind doth sometimes wander awhile."

Then again he wiped his beloved glasses, and placed them most tenderly upon his nose. "Leave it to me," he said, "leave it to me, and to woman's wit. No, I will not call the last by so light a name, for surely it is something higher which God hath given to those wondrous creatures in place of man's strength and power, to help them out of queer places, and to confound the strong."

And it was as he was bidding me farewell at the gate, that he turned again saying, "Leave it to Vita and to me, and with God's help no harm shall come of it. Volo must go on with his search, for no person can stay him."

CHAPTER XV

ROYAL GOES IN SEARCH OF THRIFT

NOW it was the month of July in that same year, that Royal Clemoes came to bide with us for a space at Trebetherick. For some while past she had been sad and ailing, my uncle Christian Clemoes being greatly concerned about her. He had come to see my mother and they had talked together a good hour in the best parlour over many things, but more particularly of the maid, that being upmost in good Uncle Christian's heart at the time.

"Now why don't you bring her here Christian," my mother had said at length, "maybe the air of Trebetherick will bring back the colour to her cheek, and the strength to her body again."

"Lord now, thank you kindly Martha," he said, "I'm darned if it baint the very thing."

But it was a long time before they could persuade our Royal so much as to put her foot inside our doors, the fear of that which had gone by, being yet so strong upon her. We all coaxed her in turn, but she would heed no word of it, till at last it took all the kindly persuading of Parson Trehern to make the maiden most unwillingly consent to bide with us for a time.

And first along it seemed as though the change to Trebetherick were but making her the worse. For she would sit by the hour at her chamber window, with her hands loosely folded upon her lap, her sweet eyes seemingly as if all life had left them, ever gazing outwards at the heaving waters beyond.

Nor could we tempt her into the garden, where my mother was giving much time to her flowers just then.

"Come Royal," my mother would call, "and help me tie up these here siny. 'Tis all fallen abroad and gone scat with last night's rain."[37]

"Oh, please not Aunt Martha," she would cry with a shudder, "I can't come just yet, not into the garden."

But Parson Trehern preached patience to us, saying that time would heal, if Trebetherick did not. So we bided quiet and let the maiden be, not pressing her to do aught to which she had no care to do. It was one soft evening I mind when the moon was at its full, that tempted by the gentle kindness of the night I left my pens and papers and wandered forth into my mother's garden. From below came the murmur of the sea, and the air was sweet with the scent of the flowers. It was as I passed along the myrtle walk, and neared the bower at the bottom, that my ears caught a sound which caused me to pause awhile within the shadow of the hedge.

A woman was sobbing most grievously within the bower, most grievously indeed as if her heart would break. I could catch a glimpse of her white gown where the moonlight partly entered; she seemed to be kneeling on the ground with her hand on the boarding of the seat. I did not like to move, in fear it might trouble her to be taken thus unawares, so bided still where I was, though not liking my position which was greatly like that of an eavesdropper. And still she lay there sobbing as though her heart would break.

"Oh Seth," she said aloud, "Oh Seth my darling, come back. Oh sweetheart, dear, I cannot live without you."

The moonlight shone fuller into the arbour, I could see her lying there with both her hands clutching hold of the wood of the seat, and her fair head upon her arm.

"Oh God in Heaven," she prayed, "send him back to me, send him back to me here. Here where he told me he loved me."

---

37 Siny: the dame's violet (*Hesperis matronalis*). Scat: knocked down, scattered.

And I heard her kiss the hard wood-work of the bench where she lay.

The beech leaves rustled overhead, the murmur of the sea came upwards from the shore; I turned and crept softly to the house, not daring to hear more, my eyes full and my heart aching sore.

After a while she flitted through the kitchen like a ghost, and going softly to her room I heard her close the door.

Now it was after this night of which I spoke aught to any person, that our Royal showed no more dread of the garden, indeed it was the other way about, for she was ever in it, fluttering from flower to flower as a butterfly, or sitting by the hour with her bit of sewing in the arbour, which before she had so greatly shunned. Trebetherick seemed to be now doing in truth that which my Uncle Christian and Parson Trehern had hoped. For the colour came back to her cheeks, and the lightness to her step, and she would sing sweetly about the place as a bird doth in the spring, songs which had not passed her lips for many a weary month gone by, the very presence of things hitherto dreaded bringing a new comfort to her heart, and a new light to her eyes.

Now one bright day it happened that my mother and I had business at Rock. We were to meet with a certain John Richards of Wadebridge. Starting somewhat early in the morning so that we might have the day before us, my mother wishing to take advantage of the outing to visit the old Miss Mably.

It was after we had gone, that may be owing to the silence of the place, a restlessness came over Royal and a longing to go further afield than just the garden and the downs beyond came strongly upon her. She thought of Volo for a moment, but put it aside; had not the folks said that for a long while past he was mostly in his boat, and that he had given up going Pentire ways altogether, so what need was there to fear. She tied on her hat with the cherry ribbons, for she was ever a dainty maid, and tripped away with a light heart thinking she would go gathering thrift on Pentire Head, which flower does grow there in great abundance and of which she knew my mother was greatly fond.

She crossed Polseth Strand on her way, gathering shells as she went, laughing at the queer ways of the sea birds, seeking their food along the edges of the creeping tide, and mounting the steep which stretches upwards from the strand, she began her climb up the grassy shoulders of Pentire.[38] Many a time she had to pause awhile before she reached the top, the stiff pull of it making her feel her weakness, but gaining it at last she flung herself down amidst the rosy blossoms she sought, her eyes wandering seawards over the level blue beyond, and maybe she thought of Seth.

It was after a while that her mind came back to the business which had brought her there, and she set to amongst the granite crags and along the edges of the cliffs to gather a goodly bunch of the rosy blossoms which she had come to seek, thinking the while how fine they would show in a certain pot of my mother's.

She was engaged on a blushing patch, when of a sudden a grey shadow fell across them, and glancing up quickly to see what it might mean, she saw on the rock above her, the last one in all the world with whom she would have been alone that day on Pentire Head.

For a moment or two they stayed there gazing into each other's eyes, she with whitening cheeks and a deadly fear at her heart, and he with a fierce triumph that at last he had got that which he sought.

---

[38] Steep: short hill.

"Well," he said at length with a laugh, "I've bided a long whiles for this, havn't I Royal?"

He jumped from the rock on which he stood, and coming down to her flung himself amongst the pink blossoms at her feet, and Royal thought of that day in the apple orchard when he lay just so amongst the whitsundays. That time she had for him a kindly sorrow in her heart, but now it was all fear, and a dread of what was to come. And she sat there silent and pale, gazing into the dare-devil eyes of the handsome youth below her.

" 'Tis near a year agone," he said, "yes near a year agone Royal Clemoes, since we spoke to each other face to face. Near a year agone since we touched hands that Harvest Home at Trebetherick. You've kept well away from me my dear since then. But I've bided my time, yes all through these long months past, though it near has made me mazed, I've bided my time and now 'tis come at last."

"Do you think as I didn't know where my bird was hid! Do you think as I didn't know as you was close at hand at Trebetherick. Night after night have I waited to see your lights out, and catch a glimpse of your face at the window. Aye and I've seen you wandering through the garden, in spite of that watch dog of a hump-backed David being for ever at your heels. Sure he'd be making love to you himself if he could be certain as that brother of his would never come back again."

He drew himself up to her, taking hold of both her hands.

"Let me go," she said in a low voice near choking with fear, "you hurt me."

"Hurt 'ee," he cried, and lifting her hands to his lips he kissed them again and again.

"I must go," she said breathlessly, "they will be wondering where I be. I must be going home at once, it be getting late."

She tried to rise, but he put his arms about her and held her down.

"You are not going home to-night," he said, "not to Trebetherick; nor to-morrow neither, no, nor next day, nor ever again. You are coming with me my dear; never mind where, you will find out soon enough, but you are coming with me for you're mine, no living soul shall share you with me now to the end of time."

Royal, poor maiden, felt her senses leaving her. The man beside her spoke as if the thing was already come about. She would never see Trebetherick again! She would go with him, with the man who would murder Seth. His arms were close about her, what could she do against him. Oh heaven! Would no help come!

She glanced at the face above her, pitiless and cruel, yet full of hungry love.

"I will go back," she cried, "you shall not keep me here! I will go back."

And she saw the sky spin overhead, her ears filled as though with rushing waters, all grew blurred and dim, and she knew no more, poor maid, for her senses had left her.

Volo gazed at her face a moment, then bending down he kissed her lips. " 'Tis better so," he said. And rising with her in his arms, he strode rapidly forward across the downs, while the sea murmured below, and the sea birds wheeled o'er head. Still did he stride onwards bearing the maid in his arms as if she were but a feather weight, stumbling now and then over some hidden stone, or slipping on the short crisp turf, which was in places near like glass with the heat of the July sun. On until he came to where the land drops down, and the grey spire of granite seemingly rises from the depth of the sea.

It was here 'neath the shadow of a mound crowned with rocks and loose stones, that he laid the maiden down, kneeling beside her.

"Ah, my darling," he cried, "I have not killed you! I have not got you at last my sweet, only to see you dead. But dead or living you are mine, and no living soul shall take you from me."

He sprang to his feet, ran up the slope of the cliff above, scanned with keen eyes the heights of the cliffs around, and again inwards towards the land. Satisfying himself that no living creature was in sight, he hastily regained the rocky knoll in whose shadow Royal lay, and flinging himself upon the stones, he dragged them right and left, till the sweat poured from his face. He worked on and on as one with the strength of madness in him, or as one to whom the rolling away of those stones meant life or death, on did he work until there was naught left, but one great slab of slate to which an iron ring was attached. Catching fast hold of the ring with a mighty effort he pulled the stone from its place, thereby disclosing a black hole beneath it, and seemingly leading to the bowels of the earth.

This accomplished he stood upright again, his chest heaving and panting from the great strain which he had just passed through, and wiping the sweat from his face, he went down to Royal where she lay some few feet below him; then lifting her in his arms he again mounted the knoll, stepping over the rough stones which he had so lately disturbed. Treading backwards cautiously he descended into the bowels of the earth, seemingly into the darkness of the grave.

Deeper and still deeper yet, he went, feeling his way with caution, yet knowing well the while each jut of rock above his head or roughness beneath his feet. 'Twas not the first time by a many, that he had trod these ways, knowing every trick and turn of the place blindfold, as easy as he knew his way about the grey house on Bray Hill.

It was after travelling this way for a while, he came suddenly upon a level space, which giving more room enabled him to turn, here he paused and shifting the maid more easily in his arms, he strode onwards into the darkness with a freer stride.

After awhile did a dim light begin to show ahead of him out of the darkness, and sudden he stood at the entrance of a great cave. From the roof of it, hung by a brazen chain, was a lamp of strange workmanship, sending out a soft light as it swung gently to and fro, making the shadows move, and showing many a strange thing with which the cave was decked. Beneath the lamp stood a table heavily weighed with tankards, goblets, and platters, all seemingly of gold; while about it were stationed curious chairs and couches, crimson covered and wrought about with gilded work, in strange and fanciful ways. Here a gold demon with a lolling tongue would form the back of one; there a crowd of angels faces, with a golden cloud to help them out. All round the place were stored boxes and bales of all sizes and kinds. Near at hand, almost reaching to the roof, the great white figure-head of a ship looked down, the face and form of a beautiful woman, gazing out of the darkness. Here a pile of oars, there a coil of rope, with bottles and jars without number; while the air was full of the smell of mould, and the place had the feel of a vault.

Volo staggered into the light but looked at naught, he laid the maiden down upon a stained and mildewed couch, then kneeling beside her gazed upon her face.

"Oh Royal, Royal, speak to me," he cried, with passion and fear in his tones.

But the maid lay there pale as death, beneath the strange light of the swinging lamp and spake no word.

He rose and went to a dark corner at the back and bringing

forth a jar from it with a cup, he poured out a small portion of the liquid and moistened the maiden's lips, but she lay there making no movement, nor opened eyes the while.

"Oh sweetheart," he said softly, "wake up, wake up. Oh my God what shall I do!" For she still lay there in silence as one who was dead.

Again he poured some of the liquid between her lips and bent over her, waiting with shortened breath for signs of life. At length he saw the colour coming back to her cheeks, and she turned a little where she lay and heaved a sigh.

He slipped his arm beneath her head, and waited quietly the while, kneeling by her side, and closely scanning her face.

Then at length she opened her eyes, gazing in a dazed sort of way about her, first to the dark roof of the cave above, then to the great white woman with arms folded across her breast, who seemed gazing down upon her; then to the strange things which showed against the shifting shadows, and lastly to the face of the man beside her.

"Ah," she cried with a shudder, "where be I, where be I."

Volo trembled where he knelt at her words, for that the man's love was deep for the maid there was never any doubting.

He took his arm from under her head, and brought soft things for her to lay it on, and leaving her side he went to the other part of the cave, thinking maybe as she would come to herself better without him.

The maid lay for a while trying to collect her mind. What had happened! Where could she be! She raised herself up and looked about her. Above her the blackness of the cave seemed as though without limit, and again beyond the light she could see naught but a great blackness, the wavering light but catching hold of the near objects about her. Her eyes dwelt on the great white woman bending over her, on the goblins and strange beasts climbing up the chairs, on the table of gold which seemed to dance before her in the flickering of the light.

"Surely," she said, "I be going mazed. Oh where be I to."

She tried to rise from the couch, but her limbs felt like lead and she tottered back again, still faint and sick with that she had passed through.

Volo came out of the shadow and stood at her side. "There is naught to be afeared of Royal," he said quietly, "and it is no use you trying to get away my dear, for you will never do that."

"Oh let me go," she cried, near wild with terror, "take me out of this awful place, take me out, take me out."

He knelt down by the side of her again, taking both her trembling hands in his.

"Where be I?" she cried, trying to drag her hands away. "Answer me that."

"In the cave of Michael Trevennon," he said with a laugh, "and a fine place it be too."

Poor Royal gave a stifled cry, hiding her face in her hands.

"Now listen, sweetheart," he went on in a coaxing way. "There be naught for you to be afeared of. No person shall come to you my pretty that I promise you. This here is the place of Michael Trevennon, I have found it, so it be mine. Now listen to what I be telling you and don't 'ee cry and shake like that."

"Months and months, Royal, have I been hunting for this here place for you, yes," he cried, " 'tis God's truth, for you. So as I could give 'ee dear just all you waned. I knew my dear as you'd never come to poor beggar Volo, but 'twould be a different thing, my maid, if I could give you gold enough to make you rich for life, and laces an' jewels, to dress you up finer than ever was the Squire's lady to Padstow."

He rose to his feet and going into the darkness she heard him rummaging and moving about beyond. She sat there shuddering, but her mind had now cleared, and she felt that her one business was to try and keep her reason.

At length Volo came back to her with a small box of wood in his hand, and kneeling again beside her, he placed it on her knee and opening the lid, drew something from it which seemed as a flash of lightning in Royal's eyes.

"Oh," she cried with wonder, "whatever be it?" And her breath came quickly as he dangled the wondrous thing before her eyes.

"That," he said, while his eyes glowed with a strange light, "that thing in itself be worth a king's ransom. And it be yours my pretty, yours to hang about your lovely neck. Yours when I dress you in velvets an' silks, with a queen's palace to live in. There now let me put it on for you!"

"No, no," she cried shrinking back, "it be not yours, Volo. It is evil, it be not yours. You shall not do it, Volo."

"Not mine," he shouted, "when I've toiled and sweated all these months to get it. Not mine. It be mine, all, all mine. I'd like to meet the man as would say it wasn't. I'd pretty quick stick my knife in him," and he laughed an ugly laugh.

And Royal as she looked saw the same face before her, as had gazed into her eyes that night through the trellis work of the jasmine bower at Trebetherick. And with the thought of it a curious calm came upon her, and a clearness of thought and purpose along with a sudden strange strength.

"Put it round my neck, Volo," she said bending forward, "of course it be yours if you found it."

Volo looked hard at her for a moment or so. He was puzzled by this strange change in her ways. Ah! he thought to himself, all maids be the same, the glitter of a bauble will win them, when a man's love can find no footway.

She bent her head as he fastened the snap of the thing behind, then he stooped and kissed the white neck he had touched, and standing back a pace he gazed at her where she sat with that wondrous thing on her breast, glittering and glistening as liquid fire as her bosom rose and fell.

"Ah my beauty," he cried, and flinging his arms about her he did kiss most passionately her lips, her eyes, her hair, and held her to him as though he would never let her go.

"Volo," she said quietly, "now you must not do that any more, for you frighten me, and if you do frighten me so, why then of course I shall not want to stay with you."

Volo let go his hold of her, and looked upon her face. What was the meaning of this strange change in the maid. Was it but the glitter of the bauble which had got the hold of her, and dazzled her eyes, or was it that great thing come to him at last which he would have given all the wealth of Michael Trevennon's cave to gain?

Royal looked up at him, smiling sweetly the while. "Now no more of that nonsense to-night Volo," she said, "that is to say if you really love me."

"If I love you," he cried. "Oh little sweetheart but you surely know it."

"Why of course I do," she said with a little laugh.

"Ah," he cried, with a tremble in his voice, "I will take you away, darling, far across the sea to foreign lands. Far away from this damned coast, far, far away, my birdie. There you shall be a queen, my dear, and have all a man can give, Royal. All a man can give."

The maid shivered where she sat, but smiled in his face the while.

And on and on he talked as they sat there, strange, wild talk, of far off lands with flowers and sunshine, such as she had never dreamed of, talked and talked as the hours went on, content to see her face but raised to his, and the smile upon her lips.

"Damn," he said at length, "it be getting late my maid, and I must leave you."

"Leave me," she cried clasping her hands as though in fear, "Oh Volo!"

"No need to be afeared, my sweet," he said. "I shall be back afore morning. But those sharp eyes of Vita's would be after me if I did not get home before midnight. An she knows as my boat be moored to Michael Trevennon's steps."

"Now," he went on, "there be both meat and drink for you; I ever keep somewhat about, not knowing but what some day I may be trapped as a rabbit in its hole. But it baint very likely," he added with a laugh.

He brought bread, meat and wine, placing it on the couch beside her.

"Now let me see you eat a bit afore I go," he said.

And the maid made a pretence to do so, as he asked her, taking a sip or two of the wine, knowing she would be wanting all her strength to go through with that which was before her.

"Now," she said, "you really need not be waiting, Volo, I shall be getting on very well, for indeed I be real hungry."

He brought her a warm blanket, and told her to wrap it about herself if she felt the cold. Then standing he watched her as she sipped the wine, as though loth to go.

"Royal," he said hoarsely, "I wonder if you know how much

I love 'ee." He bent down quickly to her. "One kiss my dear," he whispered, "before I go."

She lifted up her lips to his and kissed him on the mouth.

He turned quickly on his heel and left her, not daring, if but for a moment longer, to trust himself in her sweet presence, fearing he might undo by some wild words all that which he had gained. And the maid sat there holding her breath as she heard him go stumbling away into the great darkness beyond.

I must listen, listen, she thought, which way! which way!

Fainter and fainter grew the sounds of his footsteps, and at length they did altogether cease, and the silence of the grave was about her, and the poor maid sat there with the glittering things upon her breast, as one turned to stone. Alone in that ghastly place of which no human being knew, saving that one who had but left her.

Alone, alone in the cave of Michael Trevennon. And a deadly fear of unknown things came upon her.

She took the glittering thing from her neck and laid it in the box.

"And now God help me," she said.

CHAPTER XVI

HOW VITA WENT IN SEARCH OF ROYAL

NOW that same night, when the dusk had fallen and the stars were beginning to show, the maid Vita was sitting alone on the stone wall outside the house on Bray Hill. The tide came merrily in bringing the small craft along with it, on their ways upwards to Padstow Harbour beyond.

The maid sat watching them, as they glided swiftly by she could hear the voices of the sailor-men calling one to the other as they passed, and the flap of the sails as the breezes made a catch at them.

Below her, at the foot of Michael Trevennon's steps Volo's boat lay moored, straining at the rope which held it, the wavelets sucking against the keel of it as it rocked to and fro with the tide.

Where was Volo now, she wondered, it was getting late, and the supper spoiling in the pot.

She sat awhile pondering on his strange ways, when the sudden click of the garden latch made her turn about, and looking up she saw the tall figure of my mother in front of her.

She started to her feet with a cry of surprise, for never before had Martha Rounsevall so much as put her foot inside the walls of Michael Trevennon's place.

My mother laid a trembling hand upon the maiden's arm, twice she tried to speak, but no words came to her, then near choking she cried, "Vita, where be Royal?"

The maid's heart near stopped at her words, and she looked at my mother with scared eyes.

"What do you mean, Martha Rounsevall?" she said.

"Where be Royal Clemoes," my mother said again, gripping

tight hold of the maiden's arm as she spoke, so as Vita almost cried out with the pain of it.

"Listen! she has gone, gone do you hear. She baint at Trebetherick, we have searched everywhere, sand hills, strand and rock. Her baint nowheres," she gasped.

Vita saw terror grow in my mother's eyes, and her heart stood still at the thought which came to her mind, but she spoke naught, but stood still waiting for my mother to go on.

"She's been missing from noon this day, and she scarce outside Trebetherick doors this three weeks past, and now it's come dusk and the maid still out on the wanders. "Where be she?" she cried, shaking the maiden's arm as she spoke. "Tell me that at once."

"She be not here, Mother Rounsevall," Vita answered slowly, "for I have not set eyes on her this day."

" 'Tis ontruth which you speak," cried my mother near beside herself, "you've got her here sure enough, in this evil house of yours. Give her up at once, do you hear me; give her up."

Vita dragged her arm away from my mother's hold, and drawing herself up to her full height, laid her two hands upon my mother's shoulder, and looked down steadily into my mother's eyes.

" 'Tis truth, and no ontruth which I be telling," she said, "the maid be not here. Rest a bit mother, and hearken to me."

She made my mother who was one tremble from head to foot sit her down upon the wall, and she stood the while quietly by her side, turning quickly over in her mind that which was best to be done.

"You must go home," she said at length, "go back to Trebetherick. You can say as Vita has gone to look for Royal. For I be just the one as knows the places as Royal takes pleasure in. That I bring Royal Clemoes back to you this night without harm or hurt, I promise you, Mother Rounsevall, and if I do not . . . . , " and the maid stopped short in her speech, and looked outwards across the Bar. "But I will," she said, turning quickly round, "bring her back to you this night without harm or hurt."

And my mother looking upwards saw a strange look of power and strength upon her face, for now that her passion had gone from her my mother felt the weakness as of a child come over her.

"Oh let us go at once Vita," she said trembling, "let us go at once."

Vita went swiftly into the house, and fetching her long dark cloak threw it around her, pulling the hood of it over head.

"I be ready," she said, "I will go with you on the ways as far as Trebetherick gate."

My mother let her take the lead, following as quickly as she might after, thankful for the strength of the maid, with a feeling that she would bide by her words, if she died in the doing of it.

They spake no word to each other till they came to Trebetherick gate.

"Good night, Mother Rounsevall," said Vita in the same quiet voice she had used the whole way through. "Have no fears, I will bring her back this night to Trebetherick."

"God grant as our words may be true," my mother made answer with tears in her eyes. "For how can I face Christian Clemoes if aught happened to Royal through her stay with us of Trebetherick."

"I will bring her back this night," cried Vita, with a strange look in her eyes, "or I never see Trebetherick again."

And with the words she drew her cloak the more closely about her, and went forward into the dusk as a flitter-bat into the night.

She made her way inland from Trebetherick keeping high above the little hamlet of Polseth, and crossing the brook in the combe, leaving the sands to her left, sped quickly up the steep cleve, and so onwards over Pentire Glaze. Now and again she crouched low behind some bush or bunch of furze holding her breath the while, listening and peering with her eyes as keen as steel into the dim light beyond.

But she neither heard nor saw aught that made her stay on her way for long. On, on she went flying swift as a night bird under the silent stars across the open downs, with the wash of the sea below her, on, on, till she came to Pentire Head, and at length stopped breathless and panting above the great stone which Volo had so lately rolled away.

"My God," she muttered, "he be there sure enough. It be as I thought. Then stooping she peered into the black depths below. And so for a few moments she bent and listened for any sound which might come to her ears, but all seemed still as death.

"I must wait," she muttered, and creeping down into the shadow of the knoll, she laid herself down upon the grass wet with dew, and bided her time.

And so she stayed for a while listening with all her senses, but she heard only the murmurs of the sea, or the cry of some lonely sea bird winging homewards through the night. The cold dews made her limbs feel cramped and stiff, she shifted her place a little and stretched out her hand to steady herself, when she touched something strange which had not the feel of the turf in it, and catching hold of the same she knew it for Royal's hat with the bunch of cherry ribbons. Her breath came short and quick. She was right, she would find her! Not only was Volo below but the maid she sought along with him. And she clasped more closely to her the ribbons of Royal's hat.

Sudden she heard a sound above her, as of one treading and

slipping upon round stones. She dared not look upwards, but crept the closer under the shadow of the knoll, then came the panting breath of a human creature and the heavy thud of a great stone as it dropped into its place.

"Sure she be safe now, same as if she lay in her grave," muttered a voice that she knew for Volo's, "no need to put the rest back to-night. I must be back again early before dawn."

Vita lay still and held her breath, the next few moments would mean all to her. Which way would he go! Most surely if he came this side of the knoll he must see her, and then all chance of her finding Royal, and keeping her word to Mother Rounsevall would be over.

Volo stood for a bit kicking the loose stones over the slab, then turning sharply about made straight for the steep cleve behind him. She could see him now as he climbed as a dark shadow against it, and at length his whole form, black and straight against the starlit sky where it cut the edge of the cleve. There he stopped and looked about him. Oh Heavens would he see her. She dropped her face under her dark hood flat upon the turf daring to look upwards no more.

After a while she found courage enough to lift the corner of her hood and gaze upwards at the cleve above her, but its black line was clear, and she heard no sound of any living thing about her. Raising her cramped limbs slowly she drew herself together, and pressing her hand to her throbbing temples tried to think on what next she had to do.

She rose from her place and crept slowly up the track which she had seen Volo take but a short while before, and gaining the crest of the cleve she had a full view before her of the slope of land which lay between her and the sea. Crawling low in fear that

Volo might catch her form against the sky she gazed into the dark beyond and listened with all her senses. but naught did she hear. He had gone, most surely gone, and should be by this time halfways across Polseth Strand.

Now, now was the time, and slipping, sliding, tumbling, she reached the rock-covered knoll, and flinging herself upon her knees on the rough stones she gripped with both hands at the iron ring of the great slab of slate, which Volo had dropped but a short while before over the cave of Michael Trevennon.

But strain and pull as she might in no ways could she move it.

Again and again she pulled till the veins stood out on her brow and beads of sweat upon her face.

"I will do it. I will do it," she said fiercely, and she flung right and left the loose stones Volo had kicked upon it, and tore at the mould and turf about the stone as one possessed. Then setting her teeth together and putting the whole strength of her young body to the work, she again gripped the iron ring with both her hands and tried to lift the great stone, which was burying Royal Clemoes. But it was all to no avail for never an inch did it move, and she sank upon the ground as one wild with despair.

Again she tore at the turf and mould about it, as a terrier dog will with the scent of a rabbit in his nose, till the blood ran from her hands from many an ugly cut, but the maid took no heed of it. She had passed her word to mother Rounsevall and naught should stop her, not if she had to dig inch by inch to where Royal lay buried.

"Oh what can I do," she cried, "there must be some other way. What Volo can do, I can do. What did the parson say."

She stayed for a moment upon her knees pondering deep. Then setting herself upon the ground she placed her feet against the near edge of the stone, and pulling steadily towards her she felt the great slab move. Slowly, slowly it began to move, till at length it stood upright above her in the groove which had been made for it.

"Thank heaven," she murmured, "sure it be come at last."

She gave a push to the stone, but it stayed steadily upright where she had raised it, and slipping into the black hole beneath, she went downwards into the dark.

She had been there but once before, and that with a guide, she felt her ways as she went but the maid was in haste, and many a time she bruised herself badly against some jutting rock, or knocked her head against a bit lower than she knew.

"Parson saith, keep straight," she murmured, "nor right nor left nor right, nor left, sure if I did I would get into trouble."

On, on she went taking no heed of her hurts or her pain till she came to the level space, and the light began to show out of the darkness.

"Royal," she whispered hoarsely, "Royal Clemoes, where be you to."

But no answer came to her call, and she pressed onwards the more quickly towards the light.

"Royal," she called again more loudly as she neared it, "Royal Clemoes be you there." But again no answer came to her out of the stillness, and the maid near choked with fear ran swiftly on her way taking no heed of knocks or blows till she found herself in the cave of Michael Trevennon.

There still on the couch and staring wild the way which Vita had come, sat Royal Clemoes, her pretty mouth was open and her breath came in strange short gasps, each one as with a sob.

Poor maid, she had heard the voice calling her name but had not know it, the mind of the maid was that wrought up with all she had passed through, that she thought as the great white woman above her had at last taken to speech. But as Vita stepped into the light she gave a loud cry, and flung her arms out to her.

"Ah," she cried, "you have come, come to save me."

Vita ran to her side and seeing how it was sat down beside her, and drawing the maiden to her laid her head upon her breast and held her so.

"There, there," she said, rocking to and fro as a mother with her babe, "there, there, don't you be afeard! Sure 'tis truth, dear heart, Vita's come to save 'ee."

They stayed awhile so till Royal's sobbing breath grew more even and raising her head at length she looked at Vita, then gazing upwards her eyes caught those of the great white woman looking blindly down upon her.

"Who be she?" she cried, "who be she, and with a shudder she hid her face again on Vita's breast.

"Naught to be afeared of," said Vita, "only some poor dumb image with no sense in it. Come, my maid, we must be going, for I have sworn to Mother Rounsevall to take you home this night."

"Oh let us go," said Royal, "now to once Vita, out of this evil place. He, he," she cried, "may come back and then what should we do."

Vita put her arms about the maid and drew her along with her out of the cave of Michael Trevennon. Onwards and upwards they went through the darkness, pausing now and again, though not for long, for Royal to gain her breath, but Vita all the whiles with her ears and eyes as keen as a wind-hover on the watch. On they went through the gloom, stumbling but taking no heed of their knocks, their one thought to get upwards and out of the fearsome place.

At last they felt the fresh breath of heaven upon their brows, and the soft feel of the scented turf beneath their feet, and once more they stood on Pentire Cleve with the sound of the sea in their ears.

"Sit a moment Royal," said Vita, "while I drop the stone in its place; sure it be better so, he will think his bird safe in the cage when he comes."

"Now," said the maid when she had finished her business, and the great stone had once more dropped with a thud into its place, "now we must keep inwards Royal, us can't risk crossing Polseth Strand, sure it be a bit further round, but 'tis safer."

Again she slipped her arm around the maid and helped her upwards. The stars were bright above so that they could see near all before them, they spoke but little, the one thought of both was to get as far from that evil place as they might. Now they were nearing Pentire Glaze, and their hearts rose, and their going became lighter.

"How was it Royal?" said Vita suddenly.

And Royal with broken voice, and many a pause, told her all that had happened that day on Pentire cliffs.

She felt Vita's arm tighten about her waist.

"You must never go there again," she said, "never alone. And say naught of it, Royal Clemoes, if you love me. Bad though he be, he is surely my brother, and all I have. Remember, Royal Clemoes, to say naught."

"But what can I do," cried the maid, "sure but Aunt Martha will question me this very night. What can I say?"

Vita made no answer and they went onwards across the Glaze, while the curling waves below swept up on Polseth Strand.

They slipped and slid down the steep side of Polseth combe, and crossing the brook climbed upwards again towards the heights above Trebetherick. Here nearing the top, they had to mount one of those loose stone walls, of which you may see many in our country, made of the big round boulders of the shore, and no pleasant thing to climb. Vita reached the top with safety, and bent down to Royal to give her the help of her hand. Royal placed her foot in a crack, and sprang upwards to Vita, but the false stone gave way with her and she loosed her hold and fell backwards with a cry. "What be the matter," cried Vita, seeing that the maid did not move.

Royal gave a little cry of pain as she tried to rise, " 'Tis my foot," she cried, "I can't move Vita. Oh what shall we do. Sure we shall never get home to Trebetherick now."

Vita was by her side in a moment.

"If I carry you the whole ways," she said, "you get to Trebetherick this night."

She took the maid in her strong young arms and placed her on the wall, then climbing it herself and dropping to the other side she lifted the maid again and strode onwards with her into the night.

"We are nearing it now," she said at length, "and Royal remember my words, you hurt your foot on Pentire Head, and that be all the meaning of this night's work."

Royal's arm closed the tighter about Vita's neck.

"I will speak naught but what you tell," she said.

" 'Twas after many a pause that at last they saw the lights of Trebetherick below them, and at length they gained the door and my mother stood before them.

"I have brought her, Mother Rounsevall," said Vita, "as I promised. She hath hurt her foot out over on Pentire Head."

My mother looked deep into the younger woman's eyes, "God bless you," she said, "for you are one as do bide by their words. And sure the sea hath brought with it a blessing to Trebetherick at last. Put the maid in the chair, Vita, and I will tend to her foot."

And Vita went forth into the night, with a strange feeling at her heart, for had not Mother Rounsevall blessed her that night, with both tears and love in her eyes.

CHAPTER XVII
THE RED BULL

WHEN Vita entered the Grey House that night Volo was seated beside the fire. A rush light was burning on the table beside an empty plate, showing that he had taken his share from the pot, which she had left in her haste above the fire. There was a flush upon his cheek and a look in his eyes, as he glanced up quickly at her when she entered, which she had not seen there before.

"Where 've bin to, and what do 'ee mean by coming in so late?" he asked sharply. "The fire was out when I come'd in and the supper gone cold."

The maid gave a quick look at him and answered back easily, "I have been down over sand-hills, Rock ways. You was such a long time about I was wondering where you'd got to, so I went to find out as supper was spoiling."

" 'Tis best not to go wondering where I be to," he answered roughly. "Rock ways or other ways. It arnt no concern of yours. I won't have you a following of me, and you'd best be minding your own business, I tell you that."

The maid gave him no words back, thinking it the wiser to keep them to herself, so she moved about getting something to eat, for the strain of that night's doings was beginning to tell upon her. But she made but a poor pretence at it all the same, and putting the things away, went upwards to her room, leaving Volo with that same strange look in his eyes, gazing into the dying embers of the fire.

But she did not seek her rest that night, her thoughts were too full of that which had gone by, and that which might yet come to pass, and she sat herself down upon her bed, listening and straining her ears for any sound which might come to her from below.

After a while she caught the sound of Volo moving stealthily about, then the opening and shutting of the door, with the click of the gate latch after. She crept to her widow softly, and saw the dark form beyond as it slid away into the dimness of the night. And she knew once more he was on the road to the cave of Michael Trevennon.

What will he do! she thought, when he finds as Royal Clemoes is gone, and some person else knows of Michael Trevennon's cave besides himself. Sure he will go raving mazed, and if he thinks as I be the one as have helped to rob him of Royal, he'll half murder me when he comes back to-morrow morn.

She stayed at the window letting the cool air blow in upon her fevered brow. Away down upon the sands the birds were calling and talking to each other as their way is, and further off she could hear the ceaseless murmur of the Bar.

"Well, she said aloud, "I'd suffer that for Royal Clemoes," while a sob came in her throat as she said it, and looking forth into the night, she stretched out her arms towards the sea, and a sound of great longing came in her voice. "Aye and more for you Seth Rounsevall," she cried.

The birds croodled and called again, and the breezes swept inward bringing with them the murmur of the sea.[39]

And so she stayed, poor maid, the whole night through while no rest came to her, for all the while her thoughts were following Volo with quick wings on his way to Pentire Head. Now sure by this time he had reached it, she thought, and now maybe he was

[39] Croodled: cooed.

dragging at the stone, would he see as any person had touched it since he left. Now sure by this he would be stepping down the passage, stumbling onwards in the dark, now he might be calling on Royal, now she could see him in the cave raving mazed, here, there, and everywhere, calling on Royal and searching for her as one who has lost his senses.

And so she waited all that night through picturing in her mind, and seeing with a painful fancy, that which was passing out there on Pentire Cleve, and dreading the morrow, till the dawn looked in on the window finding her near worn out with anxious thoughts and the trouble that was upon her.

But the next morn did not bring Volo along with it as she thought it would, nor indeed did the following morrow, and she bided at the Grey House with a fear at her heart and a trouble in her mind, waiting and watching the long hours through for his return.

And sure it was on the evening of the third day from that, that she caught sight of him, coming heavily up the pathway from the sand hills, and as he neared her and passed, he took no notice of her where she stood, and she saw that his face was drawn and set in a way she had never known it before.

She followed him into the house and set food before him. He pushed the plate aside and made no pretence of eating, but sat a long while quiet with his head upon his hands. Then rising up he wandered back and fore about the place as one who can find no rest. And so it was he stayed for many days, asking her no question the while, for which she thanked the Lord, though much she wondered at it.

'Twas after awhile he took again to his boat, putting out in the morning and not returning again to Michael Trevennon's steps till the evening fell. Of where he went or how his time was spent the maid knew naught. He ever brought a few fish with him, but naught to speak of in the way of selling, but it kept the pot a-boiling, for which she was thankful. The look which lay upon his face that night he returned from Trevennon's cave had never left it the while, and the maiden felt in her heart, that the way lay hard for them both.

All through that summer weather did Volo keep to the sea, never as far as she could tell did he seem to go Pentire ways, the draw of the place seemingly having left him. Royal was back in Padstow along with Christian Clemoes, so it was that he saw naught of her in those days, and Vita felt at rest as far as the maid was concerned.

Time went on and Trebetherick harvest was gathered in along with the rest. But there was no gathering of folks that year at the house, nor any gay doings, nor was the fiddle of Peter Pengelly called on to make us merry, my mother feeling that it would wake up too many memories, and set that a stirring which was best left alone.

'Twas so the months passed on, till the time came for the winds to blow again, and for the sea to rage and fret. And once more heavy rains drove about the walls of Trebetherick, and the storm played tunes upon the wind-swept beeches without its walls, till those within forgot the sunny summer days, with most of what had gone with them.

At this time I mind that my mother did sit many a long hour at night time a brooding over the embers, and by the look in her eyes I knew that she saw there the drowned face of my father, as he once did lay at her feet washed up on Polseth Strand. And 'twas whenever the wind did blow that she so did sit and gaze. That she was ageing fast I could see, though still upright as a dart to look upon, but her mind was getting dazed with all that she had passed through, and she would mingle the thoughts of

Seth with that of her dead love, till it wrung one's heart-strings to hear her.

"You will come again, my lad," she would murmur as she gazed far into the glow of the fire. "I shall see 'ee again for sure on Polseth Strand."

Now it was ever since the stormy weather set in that Vita did notice a strange change in her brother. For again he began those restless wanderings of his in the dusk, and 'twas always that his steps did take him through the marsh towards Petire Head, and a misgiving came to the maid, that mischief was again abroad. So that her rest forsook her at night, and the peace which she had but for a short time enjoyed did leave her as before. For she felt that once again she must be up and watching, for these had been the parson's words, and she had ever found him in the right. When she had told him of that night's work on Pentire Cleve, he had called her a "brave maid" and said many kindly words, bidding her at the same time to say naught of it to any living soul except himself; but ever to be watchful.

So now, night after night, in storm and mist, she followed Volo stealthily as a cat upon his way, not trusting herself to get too near, but trying ever to keep within earshot of his footsteps. She took forethought to cover her shoes with stout worsted stockings thereby deadening the sound of her footfall as she walked. But many and many a time did she stop in fear and dread as a stone rolled away from under her, or a dead stick snapped beneath her tread.

Now it was ever that when he did reach the marsh below, where the bull Basan fed, that he came to a pause on his road. And she would hear the lowing of the beast, with the voice of Volo coaxing and talking to him the while. Night after night did this same strange thing go on between the man and the beast, and still the maid was as perplexed at the meaning of it, as on the first night when she had seen them together.

"Have a care," said Parson Trehern, when the maid had spoken to him of the same, "now mind you have a care my maid. For if Volo once gets round the beast, an evil which will take more than your small strength to stay, will most assuredly come of it."

The parson dropped his head upon his breast, and paced awhile between the barren flower beds, while his thoughts went backwards.

"Be you ever wide awake on stormy nights," he said at last, staying his steps in front of her. "More when the wind blows heavy from the north west quarter, yes it be most surely the north west wind which bears the devil in its arms, and blows it into others. Most truly Volo treading in Micheal Trevennon's steps, letter for letter, aye, letter for letter."

The parson turned and paced the garden back and forth till his steps brought him again to where the maiden stood. He held up his hand to her, and there was a stern look upon his face, and his voice as he spoke shook with anger.

"Now listen to me," he cried, "and remember all I say. Whatever you see on such a night as I have spoken, hanging about the bull Basan's neck or dangling about his tail, no matter which, break, break it into a thousand atoms. You do not understand, you do not know, but when I tell you Vita, that every swing of that great beast's body, with such a thing about him means death, a cruel death, do you hear, to many an innocent soul, you will know, that you are doing right when it comes to the breaking of it. To think," he cried, "a harmless beast should be made an instrument for so great a devilry."

He stood for a moment his face working and his chest heaving.

"Go your ways," he said shortly, "and God be with you, for most surely do you want Him."

He turned and went slowly up the path with bent head and in at the parsonage door, and Vita went homewards on her way with her brain on fire, and an aching heart; for never before had she seen the parson so disturbed and moved, and she felt as if this unknown coil of which he spoke, was more than she had courage to go through with.

What were his words—"death, death to many an innocent soul"—and Basan was to be the means of it. Poor old Basan. Why had it ever come to her to drag him out of the mire, and she had but saved him for this? What had the parson told her to do. Oh no, she must not forget, sure she must mind all his words. What was it! Ah, yes, to wait and watch on stormy nights, and to break to pieces aught which might be hanging about his neck. Yes, that was all, most surely that was all; but how was she to do it. And the maid staggered homewards through the darkness with wild thoughts in her mind.

Whenever the wind blew after that, the maiden had no rest; forever her thoughts were full of the parson's words, and her footsteps after Volo's.

Then it came to that time of the year when the winds do blow their wildest, and a storm broke upon our coast. Such a one indeed as did break over Trebetherick that night when we did one and all hear Tregeagle call, as plain as the screech-owl cries to its mate from the beech trees beyond the wall. For three nights did it blow, and on every one of those same nights did the maid Vita follow Volo.

She knew that Basan was with him, for she made a soft call to the beast which he knew and never failed to answer as she passed through the marsh. But instead of the gentle low she expected, naught but the wail of the driving tempest met her ears. On, on she went battling ever against the strain and stress of the wind, while the drive of the sand and the drift from the sea near choked her, but minding naught but the parson's words, that she must watch and bide her time. Naught could she see in the darkness before her, but there was but one track they could take, and that she knew step for step in the dark as well as in light, the way past St. Enodoc up over to Polseth Strand.

Now as she neared the stony lane which led upwards from Granaway where the high banks about gave something of a shelter from the blast, she would pause and listen, and in front she would hear the steps of a man and the stumbling of a beast as the stones rolled away from under him.

Two nights did she follow him thus, till they went down the steep which leads to Polseth Strand. Never a light showed from the cottage windows for by that time all were abed. Silent she stepped behind them, then sped away to the downs above, that she might the better do her watching.

And there on those two nights she crouched, 'neath a scanty shelter of furze, her cloak hanging heavy about her with the salt drift from the sea. Sure each night she stayed there with eye strained forwards to where the curve of Polseth Strand spreads round 'neath Pentire Glaze.

And each of these two nights she witnessed a strange sight which made her doubt her senses, for as she looked to where the sands should be lying level and bare, as the tide was low, there swung and swayed the light of a ship, as though it lay in deep water. Her heart came to her lips and she felt as one gone mazed, for never did ship drop anchor in Hell's Bay, though the sea should be as glass, and now it was churning and writhing beneath her as hell itself.

She crept a bit nearer, her eyes still fixed on the light, and crouched beneath a dripping tamerisk bush. Still that strange light swayed and swung on Polseth Strand, for all the world as a ship's lantern will, where she knew no ship could ride. Long, long did she watch it, nor could she guess its meaning till sudden it went out, and she saw no more that night.

Dazed and cold, and wet, she still crouched beneath the tamerisk bush, when she heard the heavy tread and the panting breath of a beast close beside her. He passed so near to where she lay that she could smell the scent of his hide as he moved heavily onward into the darkness. She turned from her place and crept after him as he went. Sudden the moonlight shone from behind a cloud, and she saw him full, with Volo walking beside him, while about the neck of the beast swung and swayed as a maiden's locket, naught but the horn lantern which was kept hanging behind the door.

Then she sped homeward by the shorter way, not daring to stop or think, for all depended on her reaching home before the return of Volo. She scarce had got to her room, and taken her dripping shoes from off her feet, than she heard the tramp of his steps below upon the floor. She lay there on her bed, now trembling with cold, now fevered with heat, till she heard him stumbling upward to his room, and she knew by the way he came that he had been drinking, which he had greatly taken to of late.

And all that night she lay tossing hither and thither, wondering in her mind that which was best to do. Oh Basan, she moaned to herself, you shall not be the means of it. She scarce knew what she was doing poor maid, for her body and brain were in a fever, and she felt dazed and strange, as she had never felt before. Towards morn when the lights began to dawn she raised herself up in bed and pushed back the long, damp lock from her brow.

"I will do it," she said to herself, "I will do it. Sure there is naught else to be done. Oh! Basan, to think I should have saved you for this! Sure more will be broken to pieces than the horn lantern about your neck. Oh Basan! poor old beast." And she flung herself down with her face to the pillow, and cried as he had never done before.

Again on the following night did she follow Volo and the bull, for again the wind blew, and the storm drove with the same fury as before. Her limbs ached, and her brow and cheeks burned with the fever within her, but still she went onwards after them till she once more came to the open downs, and the clump of tamerisk trees. There again she crouched and watched, and again she saw the swinging light up on Polseth Strand. Twice did it go the length of the strand and twice did it return. Low she lay with panting breath and beating heart, watching the glow as it swung. Then raising herself up and holding both hands tight against her breast, she sent forth a strange, clear cry into the night, which the drive of the wind took from her and carried along with it.

Still standing thus with her whole soul in her eyes she watched the light, but it seemed to go steadily away from her, once more across Polseth Strand. "It did not reach him," she muttered, "no it did not reach him, that time."

Again she gave the same strange call as loud as her throat could give it, and as she stood with straining eyes, she saw the light stop short, then swing back and forth as though jerked from side to side, and then most surely was it moving quickly towards her. Yet once more again she gave her strange clear call, then sinking down upon the turf, she hid her face in her hands.

"He is coming," she cried, "he is coming. Oh Basan! Oh Basan! what have I done."

She raised her head and again looked forth, yes, the light was coming nearer and nearer, the faithful beast had heard her call, and was coming to is as he ever did; nearer, nearer it came, then sudden she saw it no more, and through the storm there swelled a mighty roar, as of a beast in mortal fear. Again and again came the mighty bellow, sounding through all the tumult below, and then no other sounds but of the driving winds, and the churning of the surf on the rocks in the bay below.

The maid stood as one turned to stone. "I have drowned my good beast in the quicksand. Sure I have followed the parson's words."

And turning homewards she staggered through the night, sad and heavy at heart, yet making out the while that which should be done on the morrow, so that Volo might say naught to her of her doings in that night's work. Sure he must have heard the call, she thought, sure he must have known it. What could she do or say to deceive him, and 'twas with throbbing brow and aching limbs, she reached the Grey House that night.

CHAPTER XVIII
THE BLOOD RED SHIP

IT was known all over our parts and Polseth way the next morn, that the bull Basan was missing and nowhere to be found, for Vita had been up the first thing to Trebetherick, asking if we had seen or heard aught of him, but gathering no news had sped onwards to Polseth.

And there it was they told her of the strange sound which had come to their ears through the roar and wail of last night's storm, and which most of the folk had put down in their mind to naught else but the cry of Tregeagle, not daring to stir from their beds through their fear of the same.

But now she spoke, sure John Trewhit had said it might have been the cry of some beast in deadly peril. The sound had come from the strand and maybe it had strayed there, coming by its end in the shifting sands which lie close against the rocks. He could mind a heifer of Farmer Coats as had done the same, not so long agone.

My mother met the maid at the gate on her backward way, her steps dragged heavily, her face looked haggard and wan, while her eyes shone bright with the fever which was within her.

"You look properly bad," my mother said, "sure you be a foolish maid, Vita, to take the losing of the beast so much to heart."

Vita flung her head back with a laugh.

"I've lost him for sure," she said, "poor Basan! he was born to be drowned in the mixen after all, Mother Rounsevall," and again she laughed, with the tears stood in her eyes.

"Her be a queer maid," my mother said after to Honor Higgs,

"who'd have thought as she would have set so much store on the beast. Well there's no understanding some."

"No, that there baint," said Honor with a sniff and a grunt, "and you hant come to the end of her queer ways yet, you may depend."

Vita went on across the sand-hills dreading in her mind her meeting with Volo. She had left him abed that morn, when she came away, and her one thought since last night's doings had been, that she must be ready and before-hand with him against his questionings.

She found him with his hands out-spread before the fire which he himself had kindled upon the hearth. As she stepped across the threshold he cast a sharp glance upon her from under his brow, taking in her dragging steps, her flushed cheeks and the brightness of her eyes.

"Where 've bin to?" he asked her shortly.

"Basan's gone," she answered back, not seeking his eyes, "I can't find him nowheres, folks say as they heard him calling last night on Polseth Strand."

Again he cast a sharp look at her from beneath his brows.

"Where was you to last night?" he said.

Vita turned herself slowly round and looked him full in the eyes.

"Where was I to?" she cried with uplifted brows and a voice of surprise. "Where should I be but here, I'd like to know, I baint one who cares to go on the wanders through such a storm as last night if you be."

Volo drew his eyes away from hers, and made no answer to her words, but a black look came over his face, as he sat cowering over the fire, opening and shutting his hands the while, as he held them to the blaze; while the maiden with all her limbs aching and fever within her veins, set herself about the boiling of the kettle, and the setting out of a meal.

"Basan be gone," she said at length when they were seated, "I've asked for him everywheres, but no person hath seen aught of him. They of Polseth think as they heard his cry last night, I reckon he strayed that way."

Again did Volo look at the maid, long and searchingly. Much would he liked to have known what was passing in her mind, and how much she knew. But he could make naught of her, so they ate their scant meal in silence, the maid being thankful for the same.

Volo rose form his chair and reached for his hat.

"I reckon as Basan strayed to the sands and got lost," he said, "as the Polseth folks have told."

"I reckon 'twas so," she answered as she gathered the plates together.

Volo swung out of the door, banging it hard behind him, and Vita saw him no more that day.

The maid sat for many hours after he had gone, her body weary and her mind worn out with that she had gone through. She knew now that Volo had heard the call, and that he had the knowledge that she knew of his evil doings, and was feared of her through the same knowledge. What was she to do next, must she still go on lying and watching to the end. She laid her head upon the table, and the tears came to her eyes, there was no more reason in Mother Rounsevall dragging her from the sea, than in saving poor Basan from the mire! No more use whatever. And striving and calling through all her thoughts, came the cry of the beast in his peril.

"If only Parson would come," she cried, "sure I'll go mad if he don't."

As if at her words the latch lifted and Parson Trehern came in.

"Oh Parson," she cried starting up from her seat.

The parson came straight to her and took her hand. "Sit down my child," he said, "you are burning with fever! Wait now, for I know all about it," and he laid a gentle hand upon the dark coils of her hair.

"Brave maid," he said at length, "so more than the lantern had to go."

"Aye," she said looking up at him, "more than the lantern, Parson, for I brought the beast to his end by the call of my voice, do you hear, Parson, the call I taught him to love." And a shiver went through her limbs as she spoke.

Again the parson gently stroked the dark young head, as a father might his child's.

"Be this thought a comfort to you child, that you know not how many human souls you have saved through that same call."

"Be that so?" she said looking up.

"Yes, it is so," he answered, "most surely so. Basan was being used for evil ends; for a while that is stopped, and by your brave call, my child, which cost you so much. Now rest awhile for you have need of it. But when the wind blows it is still needful for you to be awake; that which Volo hath in his mind has not left it, though Basan be buried in the sands. He will find ways and means, my maid I fear, and none but you have the power to watch his doings."

"Oh Parson," she moaned, "how will it end."

"That is more than I can say," he said, "the ways of the Lord are passing strange."

Now for a time the winds lulled and gave way to a cold driving rain which swept against the windows of Trebetherick for many day without ceasing, then again did the winds arise with all their clamour and fierceness more strongly than before. And I noticed that the restlessness which ever overtook my mother at the sound of it, was upon her once again, and more strongly than I had heretofore seen it. Again and again she would rise from her chair, and opening the door stand there peering into the darkness, as if listening for some sound which must come to her through the screech and roar of the storm. Then as she closed the door she would mutter to herself, "Not yet, not yet, but it will come; that which I wait for will most surely come."

"Her's hearkening for Tregeagle," Honor would say under her breath. "Lord save us of Trebetherick from ever hearing the screech of un again."

Whether it was that sound or another which my mother listened for so intently I cannot say, but most surely, on that night of strange and terrible happenings which was to bring with it both joy and sorrow to Trebetherick, did my mother suddenly raise her eyes from her knitting and with uplifted hand call on us to hearken.

The storm was raging its loudest without and we had none of us heard aught but the howl of it for many an hour past. But we of Trebetherick knew of this strange power of my mother's, and as she bade us hearken, we did so, holding our breath and listening for that which she expected.

"I hear it," she cried, "I hear it."

And most surely as she spoke, through the howling of the tempest there rolled upwards from the sea, that same full booming sound which Seth and I had hearkened to so many years agone, as we sat shivering and terror struck, at we knew not what, on the settle of that same kitchen of Trebetherick.

My mother clasped her hands together and looked straight before her with a strange, fixed look in her eyes.

"It hath come at last," she murmured, "I shall meet him yet once again on Polseth Strand."

And after her words all seemed to happen over again once more, as it did that night near twenty years agone when we sat with the blood running chill in our veins, with the cry of Tregeagle in our ears. It seemed as if I were but a slip of a lad again, only that Seth was not there to keep me company. For there was Honor already warming the blankets at my mother's orders, and Anthony busy with the lantern and my mother herself with set lips and white face, busy with the basket of cordials.

And all the while, mid the thunder and striving of the storm, the low booming of the guns swelled upwards from the sea.

"Come," my mother said at length as she tied her black hood tightly beneath her chin. "Bring the light, Anthony Guy, I be ready."

"Which way be the sound," she asked, as we paused a moment outside the door mid the rush and roar of the tempest.

And again it rolled upwards on the wind as if in answer to her words.

" 'Tis Polseth way," said Anthony Guy, "there's no mistaking that. Lord have mercy on Trebetherick. Polseth way again."

My mother spoke no more, but gathering her cloak more closely about her strode forward into the blackness of the night, we following as quickly as we might up the stony lane which leadeth to the village of Polseth. Gaining the higher land, the more did the full sweep of the tempest strike upon us, the salt foam clinging against our eyes and lips, near blinding and drowning us the while.

The folk were already out on the cleve, with Parson Trehern in their midst, his hat tied tightly on with the help of his bandanna, and a horn lantern in his hand.

"They be doomed for sure," John Trewhit was shouting as we neared them. "They be well in the bay by the sound, and naught can save them, for the night's as black as hell."

My mother drew herself up, and a wild look came to her eyes, I could see her face by the light the parson held.

"You lie, John Trewhit," she said, "my Seth will come home to-night. God hath told me and I know it."

John Trewhit strong man as he was turned pale at her words, and the folks who heard her looked scared and shrank away. But I, gazing on her face, feared that her reason had gone at last, as I had often dreaded it might.

"Parson," she cried, laying her hand upon his arm and gazing into his eyes, "my Seth is aboard that ship, do you hear! Sure when the time comes for it, you will help me to drag him ashore." She spoke with pleading and a tremble in her voice as though afraid of the answer.

And the parson spoke her gently in his kindly way, "Have no fear, Martha, my woman, when the time comes I will be there to help."

A look of great content came over my mother's face at his words, and she slipped from his side moving away into the darkness amongst the folk.

The sound of the guns was now seemingly nearer, and the call of them came quicker, the one upon the other, then they ceased and no sound came to the ear for a long while but the raging of the surf and the roar of the mighty wind.

We were thinking that maybe they had given up all hope, or that the sea had already claimed them for its own, and the parson was advising one and another of us to keep along the rocks, and with the help of the few lanterns we had to watch for any poor soul who with the Lord's help might have strength enough left in him to gain the shore, when suddenly out of the blackness there showed a light, which brought a cry of fear from those who were gathered around, while the cold sweat stood on our faces, and strong men's limbs trembled as though with ague.

It was a sight so fearsome and awful, like unto the which none had ever seen before, that those who read these words will find it a difficult matter of belief. But they who were gathered there that night will swear to the truth of it unto their dying day, Parson Trehern and myself being amongst their number.

For of a sudden from out of the blackness of the night and the mad churning of the sea, which had hitherto been but as a hidden raging in the darkness, there arose a crimson glow, blurred and dimmed at first, but soon to gain the mastery. For it spread abroad as we watched it, as the dawn creeps over the sky, the outward edges of it softened by the salted drift, while the middle of it grew deep as unto the colour of blood.

Then as from out of the heart of this strange thing, which coloured the sea around, we who were watching did see the form of a ship arise. Blood red were her broken spars and masts, dripping as though with blood her tangled dangling ropes, her decks streamed blood, her sides ran blood, while the maddened sea leaped and roared about her, running red as blood to the blackened rocks beyond, leaving crimson smears behind them, wherever they touched or spouted. Wider and wider spread the crimson stain, until the Bay of Hell beneath us seemed but a churning, seething mass of the same awful thing. Sure 'twas the Bay of Hell in truth. The fiery wrath of it glowed upon us, and shone in the scared eyes of the folk. The face of Parson Trehern looked set and stern in the light of it.

"The work of the Evil One," he muttered. And I could see that he was praying.

Slowly, slowly as it came, did the light begin to fade; slowly,

slowly did the awful thing sink as in a crimson mist before our eyes, leaving us again with the blackness of the night and to the raging tempest and the sea.

Then from out of the storm came a sound which chilled our very marrow, and I who had heard it before knew what was coming upon us. At first it seemed a long way off, then swiftly it was amongst us, with a cry so keen and piercing that the very storm seemed hushed. We felt the breath of it as it wailed and screamed about us, now sobbing and moaning in our very ears, then far away as though filled with a mocking laughter too terrible to hear, then once again it circled as though above our heads, and with the cry of a tortured soul, it swept away across Hell's Bay, till the sound was lost in the storm.

"Surely hell is let loose this night," said Parson Trehern in my ear. "David, where is your mother?"

I looked about me as well as I might with the help of the parson's lantern, but could see naught of her. One by one with trembling steps and scared faces the folk were going homeward, all thought of the doomed ship had left their minds since the awful sound they had heard and the fearsome sight they had seen. All knew it for Tregeagle, and one and all were anxious in their minds to be safe within their walls with the sight of an honest tallow in their eyes.

"David," said Parson Trehern, "I fear greatly for your mother if she hath seen the sight, 'tis enough to unhinge her mind; keep you along the cliffs and seek her there, and I will to the strand, maybe she has strayed that way, having that strange thought in her head which she spoke of not long ago."

Now it was not until afterwards that I learned from Parson Trehern of that which was to end this night of evil doings, for

I kept away towards Granaway, and he to Polseth Strand, so my eyes were saved from witnessing that most terrible deed, which even now doth make me catch my breath in fear, at the simple writing of it.

Now as Parson Trehern did gain the level of the strand, and felt the firmness of it beneath his tread, he went boldly forward beyond the hungry reach of the waves in search of my mother. He had seen that she had it on her mind, that ere the night was over she would meet again once more the love of her youth. Knowing too well the story of the past, with an unknown fear at his heart, he pressed forward as swift as he might for the storm driving sideways at him, now and again having to make a run inshore from the greediness of the waves. And so pressing onwards he saw before him the light of another lantern, and thinking it to be that of my mother he quickened his pace yet more, old man as he was, so anxious was he to be with her.

And that which came after, when he gained it, seemed to happen as though in the twinkling of an eye, rendering him dumb and speechless, rooting him to the spot where he stood.

For he saw by the lantern light a dark form on the strand, with another bending above it. Quick as lightning a knife flashed out, but quicker yet the form of a woman swept between, flinging itself upon that which lay on the strand. Then came a cry as though of joy and mortal pain, then the whole was hid from his sight, wrapt in the folds of a crested wave.

Parson Trehern rushed forward into the darkness, till he found himself deep in the curling tide. Loudly he raised his voice and shouted into the blackness, while raising his lantern above his head and searching for those he had seen.

"Martha, Martha," he cried, "Martha Rounsevall, where art thou!"

The roar of the sea came to him, and the salt foam drenched his face; for a while no other answer came to him from out the depth of the night. Still he trudged onwards, calling with all the power of his lungs as he went, drenched to the skin, cold to his marrow, with a deadly fear at his heart.

Just as he neared the rocks on the Pentire side, he near but stumbled on something which lay in his way, and holding his lantern above his head to see what it might be, the light of it fell full on the face of Martha Rounsevall, and on the face of another, whom she held tightly clasped in her arms with his face upon her breast.

"Martha!" he cried, "Martha!"

She looked up suddenly at his call, her white face dazed with joy.

"My Seth has come back," she cried, "I have saved him Parson, saved him, I knew I should find him again on Polseth Strand."

But it was not the love of her youth, whom she held so tightly in her arms, but the child of her love, our Seth, our Seth of Trebetherick; washed up as seeming dead on Polseth Strand at his mother's feet, as his father had been near twenty years before him.

"Martha," the Parson said gently, "unloose him, we must carry him home you know, home to Trebetherick."

"Aye," she cried, "home, home to Trebetherick."

So together they raised him up and carried him slowly to Polseth, while in the parson's heart the bell went tolling, "Not Martha but another."

CHAPTER XIX
THE GREY CRAG OF PENTIRE

"NOT Martha, but another."

All that night through, while Parson Trehern with the help of my mother and Honor did bring our Seth slowly but most surely back from death to life, did this thought of his toll and toll as the bell of St. Enodoc will when the mourners be late in coming.

It was not until the grey dawn came creeping into the sky that he came to me, where I sat keeping up the kitchen fire against anything might be wanted upstairs, and told me of the fear which was in his heart, and of that strange thing which he had been witness to on Polseth Strand the night before.

"David," he said, "there is no time to be lost, if the fear I have in my mind be truth. As soon as folks be astir, I would have you go with me to the house of Michael Trevennon. If we see the smoke curl upwards from the chimney, all will be well, but if it be the other way about, thou and I must enter the house together and search for her whom I fear for.

The parson was a hale and hearty man for his years, but as he spake these words his face looked haggard and whist in the grey light of the dawn, and I saw that last night's doings had laid a heavy hand upon him. I brought him meat and drink, and bade him eat, for naught had passed his lips for many hours gone by.

We sat so for a time silent with our minds full of that which he had spoken.

"Martha now knows the lad for her own," he said at length, "the mist in her mind has cleared away in the tending of him. Strange indeed that he should so have come back to her—The

Lord hath given me back the one—she said—most surely in his good time will he take me to the other.—She has had much to bear. Last night I feared for her reason."

And I too had feared, but the Lord in his mercy had spared us from this most terrible thing.

Slow the day seemed in his coming as we sat there waiting in silence. The wind had dropped and given place to a cold drizzling rain which dripped with a dreary sound from the window eaves without. I was glad when I heard the homely clatter of Honor's feet coming down the stairs, showing that it was the hour for folks to be astir, and that the time of our waiting was over.

"Seth be sleeping like a lamb," she said in a loud whisper which might be heard all over the house. "I reckon he's main glad to be back in a Christian bed again with old Honor to look after him.[40] Lord to think of his being washed up at the Missus' feet, same as his father before him. Her knew right enough what was coming, for her seed it all in a dream. Never gainsay the Mistress when her tells 'ee to be ready with the blanket, her knows—her doth—for sure her knows."

The parson rose form his seat as she spoke and we went forth into the cold drift together. It was a sad and dreary morning, fit following for such a night.

We went onwards in silence through the dripping rushes, the clinging sand making heavy walking for us both, till we came to the gate which crosseth the brook below. Here the parson stayed awhile hanging heavily upon it.

"David," he said, "if aught has happened to the maid through my persuasions it will stay heavily upon my soul." Then he opened

---

40 Main: very, greatly, much.

the gate and we went onwards up the path which winds between the sand heaps to the house of her we sought.

"See you ought, David, which tells of her being there," the parson said when we came in sight of it. "Maybe a curl of smoke which speaks of a fire within."

And I could see by the way his eyes sought the ground he was afeared to look himself.

But the Grey House stood as it had for many years agone, with no sign of life about it. No stream of blue smoke showed above to speak of a fire of driftwood burning within, The door was closed, while the windows gazed sightless over the waste of water beyond, still watching and waiting as they had ever done, for something they would never see.

"Man, man, what do you see?" cried the parson, laying a grip on my arm and still keeping his eyes to the ground.

"A house with blind eyes and closed door," I answered, "and naught that speaks of life within."

The parson drew himself up and gazed for himself.

"The worst! he worst!" he muttered. "Come man, come! this is no time to stand here trembling."

He opened the wicket gate, and knocked at the door. Again and again did we knock, but no answer came to our call, nor did we catch a sound of anyone moving within.

Twice did the parson lay a trembling hand upon the lock, and twice did he remove it as though afraid to enter, then for the third time did he grip it sure, flinging the door wide open, showing the empty room with its scant furnishing and the grey ashes cold upon the hearth.

"If there is any living soul in the house they would have heard us by now," he said.

But no sound came from above as of any person stirring, all was silent as death in the house of her whom we sought.

Then the parson bade me stay below while he went above. I heard his footsteps upon the creaking boards as he went upwards. Then a door opened and shut, and then another. Then all was silence, then again did his steps sound overhead, and descend towards me, and my heart beat heavily in my breast as I listened, for I knew that which he feared was truth.

His eyes sought mine as he entered, his lips twitched, his face looked grey and drawn. We spoke no words for a space.

"Boy," he said, "she is not here! She has not been here this night. We must go and seek for her you and I, seek for her on the shore."

And all that day did we carry on our mournful search, all that day long and the next. Never a heap of weed or tangled wreckage did we leave unturned, never a rock or cove where the wash of the sea came in did we leave unsearched, or was it until late on the second day, that we came across aught which helped us in the clearing of this sad mystery.

Then it was that we saw before us, a dark object lying half hidden in the sand high up amongst the refuse of the beach. The Parson at the sight of it caught his breath, and uttering a cry, ran forward to where it lay.

The parson picked it up, and then we looked into each other's eyes without speech, as we had done the morn before in the house upon the hill.

"Let us go home, David," cried the parson, "home to St. Minver. The Lord forgive me, and shew me what to do."

We hid about us with care that which we had found, and we went on our way avoiding Polseth, reaching St. Minver by the way of the combe; nor did we have speech the one with the other until we were safe in the parson's parlour with the door locked close behind us.

Then the parson took the maiden's cloak and set it before the fire to dry. "It is all that is left of her," he said, "so we will deal kindly by it. The dear maid has gone from us for ever. She has gone whence she came; those whom the sea brings to us doth it ever claim for its own."

Then I took the shining knife which I carried and laid it upon the table.

"Ah," he cried at the sight of it, "these are the witnesses. Though dumb, David, they speak with a thousand tongues. Listen," he cried, as he leant heavily upon the table, till it creaked beneath his weight, "the woman whose cry I heard that night was no other than our poor Vita, the man whom I saw strike was the man who carried that knife. That he never meant the blow for her, I most truly do believe, but for the one at his feet, no other than your Seth. It was Vita who rushed between him and took that blow, giving her life for his, brave maiden that she was."

"Parson," I said, "where is he who wrought the evil deed. For these two days naught has been seen of him. Most surely must he be brought to justice."

"Justice, justice," he cried, "what is that? Will it bring the maid back to life again; or undo the deed he has done?"

"No, Parson," I said, "it will not bring our maid to life again, but most surely it would put all stop to such another deed."

He let fall the cloak and sank into his old arm chair beside the fire, hiding his face in his hands.

"David," he said at length, "you are right. Most surely must he be brought to justice. I, and I alone can do it, for I alone do know the place of his hiding, unless it be that the sea itself has already wrought that justice upon him, but I do not feel that it is so. Tomorrow will you and I seek him at the cave of Michael Trevennon, first making sure that that is the place which holds him. Then, for I have not the strength of youth, and you alas are but weakly, we will call in the help of John Trewhit, he being strong and lusty, and silent of tongue when needful."

And so it was when the dusk fell on the following day, the parson and I lay hidden in the rocks well above the slab of stone which covered the entrance to the hiding place of him whom we sought. There we crouched through the long chill night, and for the three that came after, as dogs will watch a rat-hole, knowing well that if the earth held him at all, hunger would drive him forth at last to face the light, which thing did most surely come to pass.

For it was upon the fourth night after we had set ourselves to watch, while a young moon hung in the sky, showing us more clearly than heretofore that which was around us, that we saw the stone move slowly upwards, and the form of a man ascend until he stood upright upon the knoll of stones below.

He looked right and left with a quick movement of his head, the he came running as swift as a hare with the dogs behind him towards the place in which we lay. The parson gripped my arm bidding me be silent, and we crouched the lower between the rocks waiting for him to come.

Nearer and nearer he came till we could hear the panting of his breath, then of a sudden he doubled to the left of us and swiftly passed from our eyes as though haunted by some terrible thing.

"God's curse is upon him," the parson muttered under his breath.

And there we crouched and waited, while our limbs stiffened and grew cold watching for his return. We knew that under cover of the night he had gone in search of food, but where we could not tell, nor dare we move in the fear that we might meet him on his way returning.

"Tomorrow in the daylight we will come with John Trewhit," said the parson.

Now John Trewhit, as I have before made mention, was the strongest man our ways about, and moreover the most cunning wrestler in our parts, having wrestled with John Trefry himself in more places that one, so Parson Trehern had done wisely in his choosing. That Volo would have little chance against him was clear, save by his quick cunning, or with the use of his knife, which same now lay locked in a drawer in the parson's parlour at St. Minver.

It was as we had surmised. Towards dawn we heard the stumbling of his hurried feet returning to his lair, and soon we saw him pass beneath us with something wrapped in a kerchief in his hold. Maybe eggs stolen from a hen-roost near by, or a rabbit caught in a snare of his own setting. Again did he look quick about and behind him as one hunted and pursued, then dropped quickly into his hole as a rabbit into a burrow, the great stone swinging slowly behind him into its place, shutting him out from our eyes.

Cramped and stiff, we rose from our place of hiding amidst the rocks, and took our ways homewards, thinking of the morrow and what might be the outcome of that which we had set ourselves to do.

Now it was nigh unto four o'clock the following day, that Parson Trehern, also with John Trewhit and myself, did stand together on the knoll above the cave of Michael Trevennon, with the intent to take hold and bring to justice the man who lay hidden beneath in the bowels of the earth.

John Trewhit had been told all that was required of him and was ready for his work, though he would rather have taken his man above ground than sought for him in the cave of Trevennon. For I could see that he did not like the looks of it, when the parson bade him lift the stone, and the black hole showed beneath.

According to the parson's bidding we had brought lights along with us, his forethought proving afterwards to have been a most reasonable caution.

One by one we descended—the parson firstly as knowing the way, next to him John Trewhit, and lastly myself as being of little consequence.

As cautiously and quietly as we might, we went downwards and onwards, though now and again the silence was broken by reason of John Trewhit, whose bulk and stature made it somewhat difficult for him to descend with much comfort. At times his head coming somewhat sharply in contact with a projecting rock, it caused him to swear long and lustily, which was but a natural outcome of the same; though it be due to John's memory that when chided by the parson for his indiscretion, he contrived on each occasion when an oath was necessary to smother it somewhat in his beard.

It was so we neared the entrance to the cave of which I have before spoken, when a light showed before us, making those of our lanterns look dim, and here we paused a moment to consider that which was best to do.

"Better dout the lights, Parson," said John in a husky whisper, "us will see better without.[41] Can't fight fair with this here thing dangling in my hand."

"Listen to me John," said the parson, "give me the light, man, and keep your fists free, but never use them until I give you the

[41] Dout: put out, extinguish.

word. And mark you this, there is another way out from this place. I am doubtful if the man within knows of it, but I fear he may. If it be so you will want your lantern and a swift foot, but have a caution John, and if he flee, follow not too quickly on his heels, or thou wilt find thyself over the cliff and into the devil's cauldron."

Then did we enter the cave and saw before us a strange sight. There, beneath the figure of the great white woman, seated on the rotten gilded couch was the man we sought. In his hand he held a thing which shone and danced, dazzling our eyes as we gazed upon it. Now and again did he press the flashing thing to his lips, murmuring softly over it, then again did he hold it up, letting the light from above flare full upon it, while he laughed a strange laugh without meaning or merriment, making the blood run chill in our veins as we listened to the sound of it.

Parson Trehern laid a hand on the arm of Trewhit and took a step into the light, but the man on the couch seemed heedless of our presence, keeping on with his terrible play, while the white woman from above gazed down upon him with her sightless eyes.

"Man," cried Parson Trehern in a loud voice, "the Lord hath sent us here to bring you to justice."

With a wild cry Volo sprang to his feet, still holding the glittering thing in his grasp. For a moment did he glare upon us with wild eyes as a cat will when caught in a trap, then with a shrill scream and a burst of unearthly laughter, with one bound he sprang from us into the darkness beyond.

"Take hold of the light, John. After him! After him!" cried the parson, "of a surety he knows the other way. Quick, David, my lad, follow as best you may. 'Tis a matter of life and death."

On went John Trewhit, stumbling and falling over things which lay in his way, pulling himself heavily up and hurrying onwards after the footsteps fleeing in front of him; on went Parson Trehern panting sorely, with I myself as fast as I might after the two.

We had now left the cave, and were in a narrow passage, which seemed to wind and twist on its way, as now and again we were brought up suddenly by a straight wall of rock making us turn sharply to the right or the left as it might be, and so causing a delay in our progress. But after a time the sound of the sea came to our ears, and the light of heaven to our eyes.

"John, John, have a care!" I heard the parson shout in front of me. And then I could see the two of them against the light of the sky, and at length when I came up with them, I saw that we stood on the edge of a giddy cliff with the grey sea yawning and churning a good hundred feet below.

"Sure," John Trewhit was saying, "he's a gone clean over cleve Parson, us shan't see un again this side of doomsday, that's certain sure."

"Lie down on thy stomach, John, and lean out over," said the parson, "and I will hang on to thy feet the while."

John Trewhit laid himself down as the parson bade him, and gazed down over the giddy edge into the seething tide below.

"There baint so much as a ledge," he said, "as a guillimot could get a footing."

"Look well to the left of you John," said the parson, sitting the more heavily on the lower part of John's legs as he spoke.

"Good Lord!" cried John now purple in the face by reason of his position, "if he baint sticking to the rock same as a limpiter when the tide be out."

"Watch him," said the parson, "and mark where he goes."

"He be crapeing, crapeing," said John gasping as he spoke,

"same as a fly up a window pane.[42] Sure the man must have toes like a cat, or be the devil himself, or he never could go through with it."

"Watch him close," said the parson. "What is he making for John?"

John strained himself yet further over the edge of the cliff, while the parson sat the more heavily upon his legs.

"There's naught but the slipper slope of grass, which breaks away from the cleve, and the grey crag for him to make for," he said, "there's no getting back to land that way, Parson. He's as good as doomed if he once sets foot there."

For a time there was silence, while John Trewhit still leaned heavily over the abyss, choking and gurgling the while owing to his great discomfort. But suddenly his tone was changed by the sound of one of his familiar oaths, which came more naturally to our ears.

"What is it, John?" cried the parson.

"Darn my eyes!" cried John, "If he hant a sprang light as a grass-hopper on to that slipper piece of turf, and now be climbing hand over hand, as though he knowed every crack and hitch of it, up the grey crag itself."

"Come back man," cried the parson, "come back. David hold on to his feet whilst I get up."

With much difficulty did John draw himself within, I holding on to his boots the while, and at length we all three stood together at the entrance to the cave, having a full view of the grey granite crag, rearing upwards from the sea, of which I have before spoken.

And then most truly we saw with our eyes that which John Trewhit had spoken. The man whom we sought, clinging and climbing higher and higher, where one would have sworn naught

---

[42] Crapeing: creeping.

but a sea-parrot could have found a footing. Over one wrist glittered and danced the dazzling thing we had watched him caressing in the dim light of the cave. Every step he took seemed to us who watched more fearful than the last, every second did we think to see him miss his footing and fall backwards to his death. But it was not so, for strange strength and the cunning which madness gives were with him. Higher and higher he went until at length he gained the topmost summit, and there he stood his lithe form clear cut against the sky, as still as a marble effigy on a tomb.

"Darn, if I had my old gun along with me, sure I'd fetch him down proper," said John.

"Hold thy peace, John Trewhit," the parson said sternly. "The man is near enough to his end without any help of thine."

And indeed as he stood on that giddy height, and gazed about him I could scarce bear to look, the sight of it turned me sick.

The sun was beginning to sink, and the yellow light of it glared on the rock and on the face of the man; he waved the glittering thing in his hand and laughed as it caught the rays. We could see him plainly where he stood.

"The deed has turned his mind," the parson said, "Volo," he loudly called, "come back.'

But the only answer was another wild laugh, and again he swung the glittering thing where the rays of the sun should catch it.

"Volo, Volo," the parson called again, "come back."

For a moment the man on the rock seemed to return to his senses. He turned his face to where we stood as though he was hearkening, then all strength seemed to leave him; he swung to and fro where he stood, then reeling heavily over to the utmost edge of the crag, he stretched forth both arms in front of him as a blind man seeking the light. Then with a bitter cry which rings in my ears to this day, he dropped as a stone into the empty space, into the yawning sea below, that which he had held so closely flashing after him as a shower of stars in a November sky.

We stood there stunned and silent, gazing down into the depths below as though into a grave; the grey sea heaved and roared, sending up great jets of foam against the grey crag which towered above it. But no sign did it show of what had been and what lay below. The sea had claimed its own.

Then said the parson solemnly, as he gazed into the deep, "Vengeance is mine, saith the Lord." Yet again did he speak, still watching the heaving of the waters far below, John Trewhit lifting his hat the while:

"Lord have mercy on me, a sinner."

The parson turned his face inwards to the cave, we following after him in silence, util we came to where the great white woman stared down upon us with her sightless eyes, then upwards until we reached the day, leaving the smell of mould and the feel of the grave behind us, as again we felt the breath of heaven blow.

With great care did Parson Trehern with the help of John replace the grey slab, scattering the loose stones above it, filling it all in with earth and tufts of weed, until it would have been a difficult matter for even those who knew to find the place again. And to my knowledge that was the last day that ever human foot did tread the cave of Michael Trevennon.

"So let us bury this evil," said Parson Trehern with a sigh. "God grant it may never come to light again to tempt the sinful heart of man."

CHAPTER XX
THE END OF THE STORY

SO am I nearing the end of this story of Trebetherick, written as it is but haltingly I fear and with little skill, as it needs must be by one who hath so small a learning.

Maybe I have seemed to speak over much of the ways of the winds, or the thunder of the sea, but I would have you bear in mind, if ye be not Cornish folk, that we of the northern coast do ever dwell within the sound of its voice. Night and day, day and night, doth the cry of it ever ring in our ears, calling through everything else. Little wonder indeed then be it, that all thoughts, all dreams, all doings, should be so woven into the sound of it.

So am I nearing the end, but for the gathering together of those bits which I have left loose. For some have gone from the story for ever, and naught but the memory left of them, while for others their story, perchance, be but opening to the sound of St. Minver's bells, but as for me I lay down my pen when the wedding bells begin.

Now after that strange burial in the sea, a gentle peace fell upon old Trebetherick, the evil which had haunted it for this long while past seeming to flee from it altogether.

For though the storms still raged at times about its walls, did we take but little heed of them, the merry laughter within shutting our ears against the sound of it, and the sunshine of our own happiness blinding our eyes to the gloom and drift without.

For was not our Seth about again as hale and hearty as ever, and was not our Royal flitting in and out as lightsome as a bird, with the flush of joy upon her cheeks, and a song upon her lips.

For I do not think it could have been long after Seth was up and about, that they went forth together across the sand hills, when the moon was at its full, making a silver pathway across the river to Padstow town beyond. Amongst the whispering rushes they sat them down to rest while they told each other all they had so long been waiting for, and so long yearned to tell. How much Royal spoke of Volo's strange wooing, or of all that had befallen her in his absence, I cannot say, but that she had told him all that was needful I could see by the deep look in his eyes as they came slowly hand in hand up the garden path on their ways home, also by the way he took her to his heart as they stood awhile in the porch, as though loth to let her go.

"Ah! little Royal," he murmured, "if I had known all before, naught should have sent me away."

Royal threw back her head looking up at him, while a tremble was in her voice as she spoke.

"That is just why I never told you, you foolish, foolish Seth."

So it was that Seth and Royal came together at last, all past sorrow being forgotten in that same meeting. No, not quite all, for though Seth pleaded sore that the joining of them together should fall full soon, Royal would not let it be. For she held deep in her heart the memory of her whom the sea had claimed for its own, though it was long, long afterwards indeed that the true knowledge of the maiden's sad end came to her, and whom it had brought to her arms.

For John Trewhit as the parson had surmised did hold his peace most securely over those strange doings which he had witnessed in the cave of Trevennon. But once was it that he mentioned the subject to me, and then seemingly aggrieved that the Christian burial which Parson had given to Volo was too good for his deserving.

"Better fit, four cross roads, and an ashen stake through his middle for such as he," he said.

" 'Twas Parson's doings," I answered. "Sure he knows best, and maybe it is that Volo will rest the quieter for it."

"Aye, aye," he answered, casting a nervous glance around as he spoke, "Parson knaws best, maybe he will, David. Lord knows, us don't want him back again."

But of the going of those two strange souls whom the sea had brought to our doors, and so taken again to itself, the folk of our parts had much to say. For when it came to their ears that the Grey House stood empty, and that naught had been seen of those who had lived there since the night our Seth was washed ashore, and the ship of blood was seen of all afloat in Hell's Bay, did their tongues begin to wag with many a strange tale of the doings and ways of those two, whom few had loved and most had feared, since they first set foot in Trebetherick.

Sure one did swear 'twas Volo himself they had seen aboard the ship of blood, and the maid along with him, together working deeds of witchcraft of which they scarce dare speak or tell. But none ever came to know the real truth of it, all through that same silence of which I have before spoken being so securely held by we who had the knowledge.

For little could Seth tell us of that night's doings that we did not already know, naught had he seen of the ship of blood, naught heard he of the cry of Tregeagle. Homeward bound he was on a trader making for Bristol town, when the gale overtook them driving them hard ashore, and there was naught left to do but to make for Padstow harbour, though well Seth knew the risk they ran on such a fearsome night, he being the only one aboard who clearly knew the way. They rounded Pentire Head in safety and as far as he could tell they were making onwards towards the bar, but the night was as black as pitch and they could see naught before them, when suddenly to the left of them they saw a light which seemed for all the world as a ship's light at anchor, where Seth could have sworn there was no place for her to be. But owing to the storm and blackness of the night he scarce knew where he was.

Long did he argue with the captain to keep straight on, but he turned a deaf ear to him, swearing 'twas a ship's light and no other that they saw, and sure where one could lie so could another. So it was they steered straight for that false light upon the shore, meeting their death with a mighty crash upon the cruel teeth of Hell's Bay.

He could mind her going to pieces and his struggle and fight with the waves, and then no more till he saw his mother's face bending over him, when he opened his eyes at Trebetherick.

Many a poor body was washed ashore, whom he had known hearty and strong in life, and was given a decent burial in St. Enodoc's churchyard, and sore did the parson grieve that she whom we sought for long and late, was never amongst them.

"Doubtless God hath her in his keeping, and given her a safe burial," he said, as we stood above the newly covered graves. "But I would have kept the place where she lay bright and fair with the flowers she loved, in memory of that she hath done. A noble soul who gave her life for another. Ah David," he said, laying his hand upon my arm, "she had her joy in death for she *knew* that other, I heard her cry." And the parson's old eyes grew dim with tears as we turned slowly and left the churchyard.

Then at last came the day when Royal gave in to Seth's pleadings and the bells of St. Minver rang out their merry peals, while the folk crowded from all around to see them made man and wife. Sure no fairer maid before, had stepped across the porch-stone and come forth again a bride, than our sweet Royal, clad all in white as she was with a wreath of myrtle around her bonnet and a bunch of jasmine at her breast. Sure the memory of the sight of her sets my old heart beating at this day.

And after at Trebetherick there were gay doings, with Honor in all the glory of her Sunday cap, bunched up with a new set of ribbons, and my Uncle Christian was there, also Sarah Richards to help mother with the providing, and all the folks Polseth ways about, not forgetting Peter Pengelly of Padstow to help it all out with his fiddle. Seth as proud and handsome as a king led off the dance with Royal, while Peter set the maids' hearts a going with no heed to the mischief to come after.

"One bride maketh many," he said softly to his fiddle, laying his head against it, "and where one boy ventures another will follow after."

'Twas after the folk had left that night and the last peal of youthful laughter had died away into the silence, I went forth into the garden to think awhile on all that had gone by, and the happenings of that day. A soft breeze came up from the sand hills setting the hollyhocks a swinging. The white moths of evening fluttered and clung amongst the sleeping flowers, the air was heavy with the scent of the jasmine and myrtle, while behind me old Trebetherick stood empty, for Seth had take her away. And I thought of the one who had given up her fresh young life, without which deed this day would never have dawned.

Vita, where was she now!

Out of the silence there came no sound but the far away breaking surf upon the strand, and the murmur of the sea.

www.ingramcontent.com/pod-product-compliance
Lightning Source LLC
Chambersburg PA
CBHW020934310726
48980CB00007B/769/J

* 9 7 8 1 7 3 9 3 9 2 1 9 2 *